THE DEMON SLAYI

Other Titles in the Series

THE DEMON SLAYERS

AND OTHER STORIES

Bengali Folk Tales

Collected and written by
Sayantani DasGupta
and
Shamita Das Dasgupta

INTERLINK BOOKS
NEW YORK

First published in 1995 by

INTERLINK BOOKS
An imprint of Interlink Publishing Group, Inc.
99 Seventh Avenue
Brooklyn, New York 11215

Library of Congress Cataloging-in-Publication Data

DasGupta, Sayantani.
The demon slayers and other stories: Bengali folk tales /
collected and written by Sayantani DasGupta and Shamita Das
Dasgupta.
p.   cm.
Includes bibliographical references.
ISBN 1–56656–164–7(hbk.)—ISBN 1–56656–156–6 (pbk.)
1. Tales—India—Bengal. I. Dasgupta, Shamita Das. II. Title.
GR305.5.B4D27 1995   94–1706
398.2′0954′14—dc20   CIP

Printed and bound in the United States of America

10 9 8 7 6 5 4 3 2 1

To our storytellers, Sunil, Biva, Surama, Sujan
and
to Ruptum, Munal, Rijul
and the children of the diaspora

CONTENTS

CONTENTS

INTRODUCTION

History

"Your feet are washed by the sea and your head is adorned by the snowy crown of mountains," writes the poet D. L. Roy. The region he so describes is Bengal: once united, now separated politically into the eastern state of West Bengal, India and the independent country of Bangladesh. Bengal lies in the Gangetic Plains, with the Himalayas demarcating its northern boundaries and the forests of Sunderban guiding its southern tip into the Bay of Bengal. A netting of innumerable rivers crisscrosses the region, the most important of which are the Ganges and the Padma. Bengal's proximity to and dependence upon both the sea and its rivers is perhaps the region's most defining characteristic. A tradition of overseas trade, fertile crop lands and a constant influx of travelers, merchants, and invaders shaped Bengal as ultimately a water culture: flexible, accommodating and fluid.

Perhaps the single most significant event in Indian history is the invasion of Aryan tribes from the Caucasian mountain region of central Asia. Although its history was not clearly recorded until the eighth century A.D., modern historians believe that the Aryan incursion into North India in the second millennium B.C. never fully reached Bengal. Therefore, the region managed to remain somewhat outside the influence of this Caucasian group, and its most significant effect, the engendering of the caste system in India. Caste, the principle of social stratification which remains intact in modern India, organizes society into four major hierarchical labor groups: *brahman* (priests and teachers), *kshatriya* (warriors), *vaishya* (merchants and traders)

1

and *shudra* (menial laborers). The rigid caste structure, which delineates one's station in life and prevents social mobility, has thus not been a primary characteristic of life in Bengal. As a result of this escape from Brahmanic culture, pre-Aryan indigenous folkways have flourished in Bengal.

However, Bengal did not avoid later foreign forays into its land. The Pathans (1200 A.D.), Moghuls (1600 A.D.) and British (1800 A.D.) all left their definitive marks on the region's history. Along with a flux of different invaders, Bengal's political landscape changed frequently over the centuries. Before the twelfth century, Bengal was ruled primarily by indigenous kings, such as the Pal and Sen empires. With the Pathans came a centralization of the Indian monarchy in Delhi, and Bengal came to be viewed as a difficult state to control. The most recent of these colonial powers, the British, not only based themselves in the heart of Bengal, Calcutta, but were instrumental in permanently altering the geopolitical structure of the region. In 1947, independence from colonial rule brought with it partition of once united Bengal into West Bengal in India, and East Pakistan (now Bangladesh).

Over the years, Bengal developed its own political infrastructure: a powerful feudal system of landlords (*zamindars*) and tenant farmers. By the time of the British Raj, this system had reduced itself to decadence. Absentee landowners who supported their lavish urban lifestyles on revenues extracted from poor tenant farmers came to be known as "Babus," and the *zamindari* system came to be associated with this perverse "Babu" culture. Although storytelling, art, music and other forms of entertainment flourished under the patronage of these feudal lords, their cruel treatment of farmers brought misery to rural Bengal. In fact, the early years of British rule brought Bengali society to its nadir. It was during this time that child marriage, hypergamy, *sati* (ritualistic widow immolation), the cult of Thagi (ritualistic highway-robbery and murder) and human sacrifice proliferated.

These extreme social ills and the influences of Western colonization proved to be fertile grounds for the emergence of the nineteenth-century Bengali renaissance. Reformers such as Ram Mohan Ray, Ishwarchandra Vidyasagar and Ramakrishna

2

Paramhansa brought about changes in education, treatment of widows, child marriage and religion. From the renaissance of social reform was born a revolutionary political consciousness in the region, which later led to Bengali preeminence in the Freedom Movement against the British. "What Bengal thinks today, India thinks tomorrow," once remarked Indian nationalist leader B. G. Tilak.

While Bengal's revolutionary efforts were instrumental in securing Indian freedom in 1947, independence from British rule was accompanied by partition of the region into the secular Indian state of West Bengal and Muslim East Pakistan. Calcutta remained the sociopolitical and cultural center in West Bengal, while the city of Dhaka became the epicenter of East Pakistan. This division had significant effects on the political economy of the region, since most of Bengal's industrial centers remained in India but most raw materials were located in East Pakistan. Furthermore, partition resulted in significant social turmoil, as Hindu refugees flooded into West Bengal, and Muslim refugees rushed to East Pakistan. Divided on the basis of religion, East Pakistan soon became an overwhelmingly Muslim nation, while India was hard pressed to maintain its philosophy of secularism. The disruption in industrial production and demographic patterns due to partition, spread over to communication operations also, as parts of both India and Pakistan were physically separated by the existence of each country.

This sociopolitical upheaveal has cast a long shadow across modern Bengali history. The experience of forced immigration caused a dramatic restructuring of Bengali society as new refugees struggled for survival and social space. The caste system, which had always been weak in Bengal, eroded even further as many Bengalis lost their roots and re-invented themselves in a new home. These traumatic life experiences found literary expression in a new breed of modern Bengali poetry, stories and plays. Interestingly, the Bengali "beat" authors had strong ties to American literary figures, most notably the poet Allen Ginsberg. Various movements for human rights also emerged at this time, with those who had lost everything demanding social recognition in a new Bengal. Post-partition economic chaos eventually

3

created an industrial recession, resulting in widespread unemployment in the mid-1960s. Poverty ravaged the region, culminating in the 1966 food riots. Such adverse conditions, exacerbated by the growing division between rich and poor, allowed for Indian communist parties to gain a strong foothold in the political arena of West Bengal.

The strong Bengali tradition of revolutionary activism emerged again in 1967, with three spontaneous peasant revolts in northern West Bengal. These uprisings of landless peasants against their landowners were regarded by the Marxist-Leninist Communist Party (CPI-ML), a maverick congregation of the original Communist Party of India, as an indication that the Indian populace was ready for a total socialist revolution. The party sent a call throughout the region, particularly to Bengali students, to support an agrarian socialist revolution in the tradition of Maoist China. Thus, the Indian Naxalite movement of the early 1970s was born in the heart of Bengal. The primary agenda of the movement was to break down the state system; its methods: non-cooperation with and armed attacks on all state institutions, development of socialist labor organizations and grassroots uprisings. Eventually, due to a temporary alliance between the CPI-M (Communist Party of India—Marxist) state government of Bengal and the national Congress Party government of Indira Gandhi, the Naxalite movement was forcibly destroyed by 1972. Since that time, the CPI-M has continued to dominate West Bengal state politics. Consequently, Bengal has remained a rebel state in constant opposition to the political ideology of conservatism and moderation espoused by the Congress Party-controlled Indian national government.

In the meantime, East Pakistan underwent similar political and social upheavals. While the separation of East and West Pakistan from India was based on religion, Bengali-speaking East Pakistan soon found itself politically dominated by Urdu-speaking West Pakistan. The difference between the two groups was not only linguistic, but fundamentally cultural. When Urdu was declared the state language in the early 1950s, East Pakistan rose up in a *bhasha-andolan*, or language-based revolt.

Although a tenuous truce was reached, Bengalis remained second-class citizens of the newly-formed country, as resources and industry were systematically drained from East to West Pakistan. Eventually, East Pakistan rose up again in the late 1960s, this time demanding national emancipation. After a bloody civil war, the independent country of Bangladesh was formed in 1971, founded upon Bengali language and culture. Thus, although the country of Bangladesh and the Indian state of West Bengal are separated by religion and politics, they are inextricably tied by their common language, history and traditions.

Ultimately, Bengal's long history of foreign invasions, social upheaval and revolution enriched the ideology and culture of the region in fundamental ways. The Bengalis, the people of Bengal, are today a mixture of indigenous inhabitants, Dravidians, Aryans, and the Mongolians of China, while modern Bengali culture is a hybrid of international and indigenous riches. A crossroads of many civilizations, Bengal has long integrated and accepted differences in people and thoughts.

Religion/Culture

Unlike many Western civilizations, where old cultural traditions are displaced by new social realities, modern Bengali culture has been built upon ancient foundations. This implies not a concealing and substitution of old with new, but rather, a fluid and permeable layering such that the lives of modern-day Bengalis are very much touched by age-old beliefs, traditions and customs. Throughout the centuries, the constant force which has shaped life in the region is Hinduism. Although numerous other religions were introduced during Bengal's history, none have been impervious to the fundamental cultural influence of Hinduism. Despite the role of Islam in East Pakistan, and later Bangladesh, Hinduism has become nearly synonymous with a Bengali way of life. Indeed, separating Hinduism and Bengali culture is an impossible undertaking.

The layering effect of Bengali culture, of the new building upon and integrating the old, is undoubtedly influenced by a fundamental Hindu concept: truth is eternal. This idea gives birth to Hindu beliefs in the unity of all life, the illusory nature of the physical realm (*maya*), and the cycling of the timeless soul through numerous births and rebirths. The principle of reincarnation is furthermore tied to two ideas that have become familiar in the West: *karma* (action) and *dharma* (duty). "Order in the moral realm is known as karma.... An act is the result of forces set in operation by previous acts, and it may also be the cause of future acts. Some of these effects will appear as causes in this incarnation and others in later incarnations" (Organ, 1974, p. 27). *Dharma*, on the other hand, implies the responsibilities and duties according to one's position in life within a particular incarnation. According to this philosophy, an individual's life is an endeavor, a striving to perfect the essential nature of self and fulfill social and moral responsibilities (*dharma*). In keeping with the accommodating nature of Hinduism, however, each person is free to choose his/her own technique toward such self-realization. The four paths of actualization that a human being can follow are set out by Hinduism as: *bhakti* (devotion), *jnana* (knowledge), *dhyana* (meditation) and *karma* (work).

While Hinduism is the most powerful organizing principle of Bengali life, it is not the sole force that has shaped the cultural fabric of the region. In keeping with its nature as a "water culture," Bengal has long accepted new religious and philosophical beliefs. Two offshoots of Hinduism, Jainism and Buddhism, made their presence felt from early times. Other religions were introduced to the region by the conquering Islamic empires, refugees, travelers and European colonizers. However, accommodation, not assimilation, was the consistent pattern. For instance, although caste mentality, already weaker than in other parts of India, is Hindu in origin, it still has permeated most other religious communities in Bengal such as Jains, Muslims, Zoroastrians, Christians and Jews.

Since Bengal escaped the full impact of Aryan civilization and Brahmanic orthodoxy, it was also able to preserve some of its traditional folkways. Somewhere between the fifteenth and eighteenth centuries, the cults of Tantrism and Sufism emerged in Bengal. Both of these religious systems afford a central place to female power. Tantrism, a derivation of Hinduism which possibly originated in Bengal, focuses on creative power. Thus, both the female and the process of creation are its ideological and ritualistic centers. Sufism, or *Sahajiya*, is a religious practice that has both Muslim and Hindu followers. The Sufi believes that the path to religious actualization is through devotion and surrender. In this belief system, the relationship between the divine and the devotee is likened to the mother-child bond. Tantrism and Sufism have fundamentally affected Bengali culture and beliefs by venerating the mother, both mortal and divine. Indeed, Bengal is perhaps one of the few cultures in the world today where goddess worshipping is still the norm.

Social Roles

In Bengal, social roles categorically determine an individual's conduct and interpersonal relationships. The significance of social roles perhaps emanates from the concept of *dharma*, moral responsibilities associated with one's station in life. Each person holds clearly defined identities within occupational, social and familial units which place him or her in a matrix of community and kinship. The individual is thus defined not as a single unit, but in relation to ever-expanding group identities. However, kinship provides the basic format for all other social relationships. For instance, friends, community members and even strangers become "Brother," "Sister," "Uncle," "Grandmother," etc. This nomenclature goes beyond mere label. By assuming kinship identities, non-related individuals take on the responsibilities that accompany familial ties.

Kinship is thus the most important element of Bengali society. Family structure is not nuclear, but traditionally extends to include complicated networks of relationships by blood and marriage. The most common family unit is the patrilineal, patriarchal and intergenerational joint family. "Every person occupying a role-set within his joint family knows exactly what is expected of him and what he can expect in a dyadic or multiple role-interaction" (Roy, 1972, p. 14).

The symbolic head of the extended family is the eldest male, regardless of age and occupational status. Similarly, the matriarch is the eldest female. Generally, these roles are occupied by paternal grandparents, who are informed and consulted on every family decision. Since their role is a symbolic one, removed from the responsibilities of day-to-day survival, Bengali grandparents play active parts in rearing the children of the family and passing on socio-cultural traditions to the younger generations. This is often accomplished through storytelling and the teaching of folk rituals. Thus, the Bengali folk tale becomes an essential vehicle for preserving customs and traditions. As a child grows into adulthood, she carries with her this tuition of her youth. For both men and women, marriage is a rite of passage into adulthood, symbolizing a transition whereby the teaching of a next generation ensues.

Thus, marriage occupies an important role within Bengali family life. As in the rest of South Asia, marriages are generally arranged by families as alliances between kinship groups. The acceptance of arranged marital partners arises from the concept of reincarnation, whereby each marital bond supposedly extends beyond one's mortal life into seven consecutive rebirths. Therefore, spouses are considered to be predestined for one another. However, monogamy was not the only pattern of marriage in Bengal's history. Polygamy was once an accepted practice, although it is not common among Bengalis today.

Women's Roles

Along with the changing roles throughout a woman's life-span (daughter, young woman, bride, mother of sons, matriarch, and grandmother), the power she wields in society changes as well. However, contradiction is integral to every social position a woman holds. As a girl child, she is less favored than her brother, yet the darling of her family; as a wife, she is secondary to her husband, yet the center of their home; as a mother, she is economically dependent on her grown son, yet the matriarch who controls his household. Thus, the construction of Bengali womanhood is inherently oppositional in character: simultaneously powerful and powerless. As a result, throughout Bengali history, individual women have held roles as religious and political leaders, while women as a group have been oppressed.

Both Bengali men and women are rigorously prepared for the duties of family life, but it is women who are primarily defined by their marital status. A Bengali woman's most important roles are with her husband's (affinal) family, after marriage. The peculiarity of the wife-role affirms her as the property of her husband on the one hand, and the initiator of critical religious rituals on the other. In the Hindu tradition, the wife is the *sahadharmini* or spiritual helpmate of her man. The *Mahabharata*, one of the Hindu epics, describes a wife's role as "a companion in solitude, a father in advice, a mother in all seasons of distress, a rest in passing through life's wilderness." The archetypal Bengali wife is the *pativrata*, a woman devoted to her husband. She is the ever-sacrificing, ever-solicitious wife who gains great spiritual strength through her purity of character. One such legendary wife is Behula, who, with her intelligence and fidelity, is able to win back her husband's life from Yama, the god of death. Bengali folklore abounds with such stories of powerful *pativrata* women.

Even more powerful than the role of a wife is that of a mother. The importance of the mother in Bengali society is perhaps best described by a Sanskrit proverb which states: "One's mother and one's motherland are superior to heaven itself." This veneration is clearly seen in Bengal in a three-way equivalence of the mother as woman, as goddess, and as the land itself. Within a family structure, the mother has enormous practical and emotional power over children, particularly sons. Not only the biological mother, but all women of a joint-family household, including stepmothers and the wives of paternal uncles, are given respect as mother equivalents.

In the Hindu tradition, the feminine divinity is dichotomized as Devi, the benign wife and mother, and Shakti, the fearsome warrior. Hinduism conceptualizes the feminine as the source of all power. However, this power is not always considered positive.

9

The goddess as Devi becomes benevolent only when she voluntarily surrenders her power to her male consort. Shakti, on the other hand, is considered the violent form of the goddess since she retains her power independent of any male god. Beyond this dichotomy of Devi and Shakti, the feminine essence is worshiped in a variety of divine roles: Uma, the daughter and potential wife; Parvati, the young bride and potential mother; Kali, the mother in her terrible aspect, who can take life as well as give it; and Durga, the slayer of demons and divine protectress. Interestingly, the latter two goddesses, Kali and Durga, occupy central positions in the Bengali religious landscape. The worship of these powerful goddesses speaks of the importance that all Bengalis place on maternal authority, actual and divine.

Finally, as the motherland, Bengal is idealized as the essential nurturer. Perhaps the ultimate testimony to the emotional importance of motherhood in Bengal is the fact that during the Indian independence movement, mass mobilization against the British was achieved by popularizing the image of Mother Bengal in foreign bonds. "We worship our mother, of abundant waters, of plentiful fruits, cooled by the breezes and green with bountiful grains," declare the words of a nationalist anthem by Bankim Chandra Chattopadhyaye. "Seven hundred thousand voices call you, fourteen hundred thousand arms are raised to protect you. With so much power—why, oh Mother, are you considered powerless?

Language and Literature

The people of Bengal have traditionally been proud of their language, Bengali. Originally derived from Sanskrit, Bengali has numerous regional dialects. Furthermore, the written form of the language has a long and powerful literary history. From religious texts to formal writings, Bengal's literature has been prolific. The most widely known author of the reigon is perhaps Rabindranath Tagore (1861–1941), winner of the Nobel Prize for literature in 1913.

In keeping with its nature as a hybrid and fluid society,

Bengal's literature has not been exclusively culture bound. It has integrated influences from diverse sources such as Urdu, English, Portuguese, Arabic, Farsi, Dutch and Turkish. Moreover, folk stories that were traditionally related only by word of mouth have been recorded in a variety of Bengali books. Interestingly, most of these stories of Bengal are non-Brahmanic in their origin, a rare phenomenon for the rest of India. These oral tales transcend not only class and caste barriers in their content, but in the identities of the tellers and the listeners.

Folk Tales

The study of international folklore has been enormously popular since the nineteenth century, and ever since then, Indian folklore has attracted great interest. However, "although generations of folklorists have recognized India as one of the world's richest sources of folk tales, India's tales remain remarkably understudied and underutilized" (Beck, Claus, Goswami & Handoo, 1987, p. xxv). Perhaps this is because folklorists have attempted to survey tales from all the widely varying cultures on India, rather than focusing upon the unique oral traditions of particular regions. The present collection is an attempt to rectify such broad over-generalizations by exploring solely the folk tradition of Bengal.

Indian folk tales are categorized by anthropologists as "Little Tradition." As opposed to "Great Tradition," which is Sanskrit-based, pan-Indian and comprised of religious texts, the epics and certain broad-based mythologies, "Little Tradition" is born from regional languages and their dialects, specific traditions, local gods and beliefs. While these two traditions are undoubtedly permeable to each other, "Little Tradition" generally stays away from epic subjects such as wars, the origins of the world, and the founding of communities. Reflecting Bengal's history of monarchy, the majority of folklore revolves around royalty. However, even when the subject of a folk tale is a king *(raja)* or a deity, the content remains familiar and the theme deals with everyday life. "The supernatural in folktales is not divine and cosmic, but magical and worldly, frequently comic" (Beck et al., 1987, p. xviii). The stories are social as opposed to ritual, domestic as opposed to public. Indeed, "most [Bengali] folk tales are intellectually sophisticated, philosophically rich accounts" (ibid., p. xxx).

While it shares many universal themes such as adventure, greed, love, etc., Bengali folklore has certain unique character-istics in both form and content. Rather than elaborating teach-ings about life through explicit commentaries and bold statements, Bengali folk tales rely on story structure to convey messages. The model is epic storytelling, in which each separate episode has partially independent status, but when taken together, they pose philosophical questions and highlight larger issues. An-other typical formal characteristic of Bengali folk tales is the heavy reliance upon rhyming narrative, poetry and onomato-poeic patterns. The importance of rhymes within folk tale nar-ratives is understandable, as poetry holds a special place in Bengali culture by itself. Since family life is highly ritualized and cyclical, there are folk-poems associated with almost every aspect of the day: waking, eating, napping, playing, etc. Not only rhyming, but repetition is also apparent in folk tales. By repeating incidents, statements and poems, the stories perhaps express universal continuity, the ever-repeating circle of life, death and rebirth.

The content of Bengali folk tales also reflects certain pat-terns. The stories are almost never about one central character or his/her adventure. Rather, they revolve around at least two generations and their lives, placing individual characters in kinship relations. The importance of the family is seen through detailed accounts of parental marriage, motherly nurturance and sibling unity. Another common feature is that characters change spa-tial and temporal realities with ease and without losing their identities. Humans may change into animals, plants or other aspects of nature through curse, happenstance or rebirth. All such rebirths and spatial alterations are, however, tied together with a thread of consciousness that lends cogency to the story.

Bengali folk stories are made even more complex by the jux-taposing of humans and supernatural beings such as *devata*

(deities), *bhoot* (ghosts) and *rakshash* (demons). The supernatural is, however, presented as familiar through comic por-
trayals as well as intermarriages, friendships and rivalries with
humans. Interestingly, the majority of these characters are fe-
males. The subjects of many folk stories are local goddesses
who provide boons and facilitate day-to-day life. Other common supernatural characters are the female and male *bhoot*.
Although ghosts seem to be contradictory to the concept of reincarnation, Bengali *bhoot* are the spirits of those individuals
who have died with strong unfulfilled desires in one life, and
therefore constantly try to reintegrate themselves in mortal society. Bengali *bhoot* come in many forms, categorized by what
they used to be in life: *shakchunni* (spirits of young married
women), *petni* (spirits of women), *brahma-daitya* (spirits of
male Brahmans), *mamdo* (spirits of Muslims), etc.

The most common supernatural female character in Bengali
folklore is the *rakshashi*, a demon who changes her appearance
to entice the unsuspecting male into marriage and thereby in-
tegrate herself into human communities and families. The phenomenon of the *rakshashi*, a creature who thirsts for human
flesh, may represent the threat a patriarchal society feels regarding female power. While superhuman female characters reflect
Bengal's long tradition of worshiping the feminine, their
demonization reveals societal ambivalence toward strong women
and the potential danger that such women pose to the integrity
of the patrilineal kinship structure. Although physically and
magically empowered, these superhuman creatures are eventually outwitted by human characters who use cunning, common
sense and everyday wisdom to defeat them.

Documentation of the Oral Tradition

The folk tales of Bengal have been shared throughout the centuries and generations. As evening falls and young eyes grow
sleepy, grandmothers gather their grandchildren around them
and retell the age-old stories of mothers and children, animals
and villagers, princes and demons. Although no one knows where

13

they came from or who told them first, the stories continue to be told even today.

The first formal documentation of Bengali folk tales was done by Rev. Lalbehari Day in his *Folktales of Bengal* (1883). Rev. Day collected these stories, "which old women in India recite to little children in the evenings," from a variety of sources: "a Bengali Christian woman," "an old Brahman," "an old barber," and "an old servant" (pp. v, vi). (This early volume was translated into Bengali by Lila Majumdar in 1977.) But perhaps the most popular folklorist of Bengal is Dakshina Ranjan MitraMajumdar, the author of the classic collection, *Thakurmar Jhuli* or "Grandmother's Satchel" (1907). It is said that MitraMajumdar heard the majority of these tales from old fisherwomen in a Bengal village. Following the publication of these adventure tales, Upendra Kishore RayChoudhuri wrote the all-time favorite collection of animal tales, *Tuntunir Bai* or "Tuntuni's Book" (1910).

The movement to preserve Bengali folk traditions continues through recent times. Due to the important role poetry plays in day-to-day life and particularly child-rearing, Bengali nursery rhymes have survived remarkably well over the centuries. Only recently, formal collections of these rhymes have been published. Another folk tradition which has weathered time well is the practice of women's rituals (*brata*), the worshiping of local goddesses. For each of these folk-goddesses, there is an accompanying story describing how the ritual originated. Although MitraMajumdar documented these stories in *Thandidir Thale* ("Great-Grandmother's Basket") in the early 1900s, that volume soon went out of print. In recent times, Ashutosh Majumdar has documented these tales in *Meyeder Bratakatha* or "Women's Ritual Stories" (1992).

This present collection is the next step in this history of documenting the Bengali folk tradition. The stories within it are compiled partially from previous sources, and partially from our own memories of hearing them told over and over again in our families.

14

About this Collection

The Demon Slayers and Other Stories is a collection of twenty tales sampling the wide variety of Bengali folklore. For Bengali children, these stories are familiar friends, heard over a lifetime from loving grandmothers, mothers and aunts. While the essential stories have remained the same throughout the centuries, the details and nuances of these tales are continuously changed by each narrator's unique voice. Rather than keeping with the fluidity of such an oral tradition, this collection bears the burden of the fixed, written word. Impairing it even further is the transition of culture and language; the adaptation from Bengal to the U.S., from Bengali to English.

In order to give this collection a truly Bengali flavor, we as authors have taken on the role of the storytelling grandmother (*Thakurma*). Our narrative voice remains interactive, much like the beloved *Thakurma*, reflecting her traditional Bengali imagery and style. Yet, our task is to make the foreign familiar; the distant, close. By interweaving Bengali words and cultural symbols with an accessible English text and glossary, we bring an ancient art to a modern audience.

The Demon Slayers begins with a popular nursery rhyme, "*Aag-doom, Baag-doom,*" a poem which transports the reader to a different culture, to a faraway land of folklore. This wake-up poem, recited by generations of mothers and grandmothers to sleepy-eyed youngsters, combines Bengali music, marriage and food imagery in a vivid nonsensical rhythm. And as every journey must end, the collection closes with a gentle and lyrical bedtime rhyme, "Come, Oh Sleep," that brings the reader to the inevitable completion of all Bengali folk tale sessions, slumber. The sing-song rhythm of this poem typifies the quiet and comforting ritual of Bengali grandmothers and mothers putting the little ones to sleep after filling their imaginations with heroic tales and animal stories.

In between these waking-up and bedtime rhymes are twenty tales divided into five sections: tales of marriage and adventure, tales of family unity, tales of cunning and common wisdom, tales of greed and piety and tales of the supernatural.

15

Each section is furthermore introduced by poems that bring out the essence of the content.

Tales of Marriage and Adventure: Marriage is perhaps the central event in Bengali society. When a wedding takes place, it ties together not only two individuals and their families, but unites an entire community toward a common objective. The stories and poems in this section highlight the importance of marriage in Bengali life. In each of the three tales, the path to a successful marriage is through a series of hardships and adventures, the vanquishing of evil forces, and the testing of the protagonists' true mettle.

The poems "Khokon's Wedding" and "Rain Song" are about two marriage ceremonies, one mortal and one divine. In the first, a little boy is sent through the rituals of marriage, including a blessing ceremony and a palanquin ride to the bride's home. After vivid details of other festive imagery, this fantasy wedding day is finally compared to the divine union of Shiva and Gauri, the ultimate in Hindu immortal marriages. In turn, "Rain Song" describes a wedding where Lord Shiva himself is the groom. This image of Shiva as the ideal husband recurs throughout Bengali folk tradition, inspiring mortal men to emulate his bravery, piety, generosity and love of his wives.

The first story in this collection, "The Owl and the Monkey," is a classic adventure which emphasizes the importance of moral character and inner strength. The tale traces the hardships of two princes, who overcome birth in animal form, parental rejection, poverty, betrayal and danger to win the ultimate reward of a perfect princess' hand in marriage. These feats are accomplished because the protagonists embody the qualities of ideal sons, brothers, leaders and, ultimately, husbands. Another common folk theme that emerges in this story is the magic surrounding the birth process, and the particular importance of giving birth to sons. Also evident is the permanence of the mother-son bond, which transcends all adversities in life.

In "The Precious Bird," this pattern of adventure leading to successful marriage is again repeated. With all the correct heroic ingredients, including magic, wisdom, patience and bravery, a king overcomes adversity to marry a beautiful princess from a mythical kingdom. However, even this most powerful hero cannot accomplish his quest without collaborators. "The Precious Bird" brings forth some archetypal folk allies: the mythical birds Bangama and Bangamee, the flying Pakkhiraj horse and the wise talking bird.

It is the cooperation of heroes from two classes which propels the adventure of "The Underworld Princess." A king's son and a minister's son travel to a dangerous underworld to find a perfect otherworldly princess. This story illustrates the importance of cunning, rather than physical prowess or social power, in Bengali culture. As with many of the stories in this collection, it is not the royal protagonist who solves the adventure's problem. Rather, the true leader is the minister's son, who possesses intelligence, wisdom and wit.

Tales of Family Unity: Bengali society is ultimately structured around kinship relationships. Unlike the West, where conjugal relationships supersede all others, the most important family ties in Bengal are parent-child, sibling and other kinship bonds. A rich set of folk tales enumerates these relationships.

In the poem "To *Mama*'s House," the special affection between children and their maternal uncle (*Mama*) is underscored. *Mami* (mother's brother's wife), the non-blood-related outsider, remains a threat to this natural family unity. In "Two Brothers," a poem about sibling unity, the importance of Shiva as the male role model is again seen.

The sibling unit is of vital importance in "Kiranmala," a tale in which three siblings fulfill complementary roles appropriate to their age and gender. The quest undertaken by the siblings in this story is to overcome apparent realities (*maya*) and attain self-actualization. The siblings find this truth when they are reunited with their parents, and the family unit is whole again. "Kiranmala" follows a common folk tale pattern whereby barren women, insanely jealous of a fertile woman, abduct her newborn children. The heroine and her brothers are stolen at birth by jealous aunts and, in a somewhat similar pattern to many Judeo-Christian myths, the children are sent floating down

17

a river. Here we see the importance of rivers, which are associated with nurturance and life-giving, in Bengali folk tales. Moreover, "Kiranmala" is a somewhat unique story in that typical gender roles are reversed; not only is the main character a heroic woman who propels the story's adventure, but the main nurturer is a father-figure.

The sibling unity portrayed in "Kiranmala" is reflected again in "The Seven Brothers Champak." Here, the siblings are so unified that they are not even allowed separate voices. They speak and behave as one, their solidarity signified by the auspicious number seven. Other themes present in this story are those of child abduction and the primacy of motherhood. In this particular tale, the seven brothers and their one sister reunite with their mother after overcoming seemingly insurmountable odds: kidnapping at birth; death, and rebirth as flowers; the banishment of the mother from the kinship group; and re-metamorphosis of the flowers into human form.

In "The Perfect Man," we again see the downplaying of individual identity in favor of familial unity. The moral of this story is that one perfect person can never exist, as perfection must come from a harmony of many. The twin puppies, hawks and princes in this tale are portrayed as halves of a single whole. The human brothers are successful in overcoming danger only through a combination of their heroic qualities; while one prince is honest and righteous, the other is cunning and brave. Only a union of these parts is portrayed as powerful enough to overcome the supernatural.

Tales of Cunning and Common Wisdom: While wit and intelligence are depicted as heroic characteristics in a number of adventure tales, there is an entire genre of Bengali animal tales which demonstrate the importance of cunning and common wisdom. This phenomenon perhaps represents the importance of human humility and cooperation with nature in Bengali culture.

"The Toad's Revenge" is a nursery rhyme about the cruelty of humans and the vengeance of nature. This vivid and slightly satirical poem teaches children to coexist peacefully with the natural world around them, while demonstrating how a collective force can overpower seemingly insurmountable odds.

In "Tuntuni and the Barber," a small bird reveals the importance of carrying out one's designated social responsibility (*dharma*) to the fullest. In addition, collective power is embodied by the tiny mosquito, who is able to strike fear into the heart of even the mighty elephant. The structured hierarchy of society, the importance of "brotherly" hospitality, the possibilities of cooperation and the power of cunning are furthermore interwoven in this charming tale. The poem of hospitality which is repeated throughout the narrative gives the story a sense of continuity and cyclical truth, perhaps asserting that the moral of "Tuntuni and the Barber" will continue to hold power even after the tale itself ends.

In "The Foxy Teacher" and "The Tiger-Eating Fox Cubs," the archetypal characters of the stupid crocodile, gullible tiger and wily fox are introduced. The harsh realities of nature are presented in a straightforward fashion, with intelligence emphasized as a necessary survival skill. However, the winner in one tale may be outfoxed in the next. A frail old woman outsmarts three vicious animal rivals in "The Old Woman and the Fox," demonstrating that neither size, physical strength nor age determine success. Rather, victory is guaranteed only by cunning.

Tales of Greed and Piety: Bengali folk tales not only recount human and animal adventures, but elaborate approved social codes of conduct. The set of stories in this section present moral dilemmas, with good always triumphing over evil.

The opening poem, "The Bride's Lament," describes the realities of a new bride and the order of her world. As an outsider to the family, she holds the least power and must lead her life within strict boundaries of behavior. Since her survival is dependent on the mother-in-law's benevolence, she must supplicate herself to the all-powerful matriarch. It is this pious obedience which is considered the *dharma* of a Bengali bride.

"The Ungrateful Tiger" illustrates that although the moral order of this world may be challenged, it never breaks down altogether. In this story, an honest Brahman is juxtaposed against a greedy tiger. The animal is almost successful in upsetting the moral balance, primarily due to the unworldliness of the pious man. It is the power of common wisdom, represented by the fox, which ultimately protects the cosmic order.

"The Stepmother and the Goddess" is a tale describing the women's ritual of worshiping the folk-goddess Natai-Chandi. The stepmother of this story represents greed and selfishness, which are antithetical to ideal Bengali femininity. When appropriately placated, the magnanimous mother-goddess protects the innocent children and punishes the guilty woman. "The Goddess of Children" is another description of women's rituals, this time regarding the folk-goddess Shashti. Here we see the results of a woman straying from the delineated path of piety, even unknowingly. The errant queen causes the destruction of her family and entire kingdom; only through penitence does she restore their lives. These two stories exhibit the tremendous moral burden carried by Bengali women. Through her piety, she is the keeper of family and community welfare.

In "How Opium Was Made," greed ultimately destroys the tiny mouse who is never satisfied with his station in life. Avarice also kills the character Sukhu in "Two Sisters." The unselfish and greedy sisters are presented as foils, with two very different outcomes to their adventures. The sacrificing and self-effacing sister Dukhu is rewarded with beauty, riches and marriage, while Sukhu charts her own downfall by transgressing against behavioral and moral prescriptions.

In this array of moral stories, "A Tale of Two Thieves" presents an interesting contradiction. The protagonists of this story are thieves, whose role in life (*dharma*) is stealing. Even when they try to reject a life of crime, they are pulled back into it by seemingly inescapable forces. Utilizing their cunning and wit, they finally manage to fulfill their destiny as thieves by stealing from other robbers (*dacoits*) and living off those riches for the rest of their lives. Thus, the moral path is portrayed by this story as complex. That is, socially appropriate codes of conduct are not absolute, but are determined according to an individual's identity and station in life.

Tales of the Supernatural: While a common theme of many Bengali folktales is magic, there is a group that deals particularly with the supernatural. In these stories, demons (*rakshash* and *khokkosh*) and ghosts (*bhoot, petni, shakchunni*, etc.) interact with human protagonists in day-to-day life. Mortals vanquish these supernatural characters only by using their best human qualities: courage, wisdom, cunning and collaboration.

The poem "The Ghost in the Tree" is a Bengali nursery rhyme used to frighten unruly children into good behavior. The "old man on a coconut tree" is very similar to the Western concept of the "bogey man," a supernatural character created to teach children appropriate social conduct.

A *rakshashi* is central to the story of "The Demon Slayers." The tale reveals that even royal lineages are not immune to the danger of demonic women, since the main *rakshashi* character is a queen, who has successfully tricked a human Raja into marrying her. Not only is this demon queen the ultimately threatening wife, who paralyzes her husband and rules his kingdom, but the Kali-like punishing mother who destroys her own son for disobeying her. While portraying the bloodthirsty nature of a *rakshash*, "The Demon Slayers" simultaneously indicates that an individual's character is not fixed by birth. Although half-*rakshash* himself, the demonic nature of the queen's son is transcended by his deep friendship with his human brother. The two princes, who are portrayed as halves of a sibling whole, fulfill their *dharma* as demon-killers through the course of two consecutive births. Although spatial and temporal realities are altered, the fundamental identities of the heroes and the fraternal love between them remain intact.

Two short stories, "The Brahman Ghost" and "The Ghostly Wife," illustrate the parallel and familiar nature of the supernatural world. The ghosts in both these stories exist side-by-side with human beings, ready to take over mortal identities at the first opportunity. In "The Brahman Ghost," a householder's role is usurped by a ghost, who slips into his life so smoothly that even the closest members of the Brahman's family remain unaware of the switch. Finally, the ghost is outwitted by a common cowherd, who uses cunning to entrap the supernatural creature

21

within a prison of his own vanity. In "The Ghostly Wife," the ghost who takes over the indolent bride's role is even better at being a wife than the woman herself. The moral of the tale is perhaps that those individuals who shirk their social responsibilities stand in danger of being displaced from society.

The last story of this collection, "The Demon Queen," is similar to the "The Demon Slayers" in that the main antagonist is a *rakshashi*. Again, we see the pattern of a demoness disguising herself in human form to entice an unsuspecting man into marriage. As in "The Demon Slayers," the queen's objective is to devour a young human male. Both stories also reveal that demon-killing is a difficult task, requiring not only heroic qualities but special knowledge; namely, the nature and location of the *rakshash* soul. However, in "The Demon Queen," the protagonists are not brothers, but a group of friends of differing classes, who perhaps represent united humanity. The heroes, a prince and princess, not only collaborate to defeat the demons, but are supported in their quest by an alliance of nature against the supernatural.

Although the twenty stories of this collection have been separated into five discrete sections, the categories are artificial. The themes and cultural symbolism in these tales overlap across classifications. Taken together, this collection of traditional Bengali folklore provides the reader with a rich cultural landscape populated by community relations, belief systems, moral codes, social rules and familial bonds.

There is one final poem, perhaps a bit absurd, that must be shared here. Although omitted from the tales in the present collection, this rhyme traditionally ends every Bengali folk tale:

My tale has now been said
The nauté-greens are dead.

Why did you die, oh nauté leaf?
Because the cows did graze.
Why do you graze, oh wan'dring cow?
The herder gives no hay.

Why won't you feed the cows, oh boy?
My wife will cook no rice.
Why won't you cook some rice, dear bride?
My baby he does wail.
Why do you cry, oh little one?
The sting of ants does pain.
Why do you bite, oh tiny ant?
'Cause it's only right!

Ku-toosh, ku-toosh, I will bite
Then hide away, out of sight.

With that *ku-toosh, ku-toosh* we are done, but our tales have just begun . . .

AAG-DOOM, BAAG-DOOM
(a wake-up rhyme)

Aag-doom! Baag-doom! Horses, away!
Gongs, drums, cymbals play!
Crash! Boom! The noisy band
marches off to Orange-land
On parrot's wing, a golden ray
Uncle Sun's wedding day
Let's go to market, me and you
for *pan* and betel-nuts to chew
A betel-worm slips out of sight
Mother-daughter have a fight
Saffron flowers bloom anew
Fresh, sweet pumpkin stew —
Little one, up with you!

TALES OF MARRIAGE AND ADVENTURE

KHOKON'S WEDDING

(a wedding rhyme)

Today is Khokon's blessing-day
tomorrow he will wed
and riding in a palanquin
past Diknagar head

The village girls of Diknagar
by the river play
They shake out their flowing hair
in the golden day

Red beaded garlands
around their necks aglow
Brightly colored saris
with their movements flow

A rui and a katla fish
swim side-by-side like brothers
The priest took one
and the tia bird the other

Gauri is the bride
beneath the banyan tree
Shiva is the Lord
and the groom-to-be

Dham-kur-kur drums roll
A wedding for all to see!

RAIN SONG

Tapoor! Toopoor! Rain drops fall
The rivers swell with tides
Lord Shiva's getting wed
to three pretty brides

One bride eats all day
One likes to cook
One bride has headed home
without a backward look

27

THE OWL AND THE MONKEY

Once, there was a Raja who had seven Ranis: Baro-Rani, Mejo-Rani, Shejo-Rani, Na-Rani, Kané-Rani, Duo-Rani and the youngest, Choto-Rani. The Raja's kingdom spanned from the mountains in the north to the seven seas in the south. His marble palace sparkled so brightly that his people believed it to be the second sun. His stable housed the swiftest horses and the most regal elephants in the land. His treasury overflowed with jewels and gold. Beside all this, ministers, courtiers, soldiers and servants filled his palace to the brim.

But even with such riches, the Raja was not happy. None of his Ranis had borne him an heir. The Raja and all his kingdom prayed for royal children to be born.

One day when the Ranis had gone to the river to bathe, a sanyasi approached them. Pressing a dried piece of root in the eldest Rani's hand, the holy man said, "Grind this root and share it with your co-wives. You will soon have sons as brilliant as the golden moon."

Elated at this blessing, the Ranis rushed home to plan a great feast. Baro-Rani was to prepare the rice, Mejo-Rani was to cut the vegetables, and Shejo-Rani was to cook them. Kané-Rani, who was not very handy around the kitchen, was to help the others. Duo-Rani was to grind the spices, Na-Rani was to fetch water, and Choto-Rani was assigned the task of cleaning the fish. It was to be a gala festival!

While five Ranis busied themselves around the kitchen, Na-Rani went to the well in the palace courtyard, and the youngest Rani went to the back stoop to clean the fish.

Baro-Rani, who still had the root, could not wait to eat it. She took it to Duo-Rani and said, "Sister, before you start crushing

28

the spices, why don't you grind up this root? Then we can all taste it."

Duo-Rani did as she was told, eating her portion in the process. Then she placed the ground root in a golden bowl on a silver tray and handed it to the eldest Rani. After Baro-Rani had some of it, she passed the bowl to Mejo-Rani; Mejo-Rani ate and passed it to Shejo-Rani; and she in turn gave it to Kané-Rani. When Na-Rani came back from the well, she found that only a tiny crumb was left. She scraped the bottom of the bowl and licked it clean. None of the magic paste remained for the youngest Rani.

When Choto-Rani returned, she was devastated to find that no root was left for her. She collapsed on the floor, weeping copiously. The five greedy Ranis were shamefaced at their own selfishness and blamed each other for forgetting their youngest sister. Na-Rani rushed to the mortar and pestle, on which a little piece of root remained. She collected the miniscule morsel and comforted Choto-Rani. "Don't cry, little sister. Eat this and you too will have a son as bright as the golden moon."

The other Ranis snickered behind Choto-Rani's back. "A golden moon! The only thing she will get from such a tiny crumb is a monkey-son!"

*   *   *

After ten months and ten days, five of the Ranis bore five radiant sons. True to the sanyasi's prediction, each prince was like the golden moon. Na-Rani and Choto-Rani also gave birth. However, their sons were quite unlike the other princes. Na-Rani bore an owl and the youngest Rani gave birth to a monkey.

The Raja showered the five Ranis with opulent gifts, while banishing Na-Rani, Choto-Rani and their children from the palace. Stripped of their jewels and finery, the two Ranis stumbled from the palace with their babes in their arms, crying bitterly. With no homes or food for their infants, the banished Ranis were forced to serve as menial laborers. While Na-Rani became a sweeper at the zoo, Choto-Rani became a rag-picker.

As days went on, the five Princes in the palace grew strong and handsome. On five thunderous winged horses, they roamed the countryside with no regard for their subjects. The arrogant brothers would plunder villages, destroy fields of grain, and generally bring misery to all. But the Raja was so indulgent of his heirs that he would ignore all complaints about them. The people of the kingdom grew angry and tired, yet were helpless.

In their tumble-down hut, the Owl and Monkey Princes grew as well. The owl was named Bhutum and the monkey, Buddhu. The Monkey and the Owl Princes grew up as kind and generous sons. They helped their mothers at work, collecting rags and sweeping animal cages at the zoo. Despite all their hard work, sometimes there was not enough money to buy food. On those days, Buddhu would collect fruits from the forest for them to eat; Bhutum would bring in his beak betel nuts for the mothers' *pan*. When the day's work was done, Buddhu and Bhutum would play in a tall palm tree beside their hut. The days went on, with the two children and their mothers living happily.

One evening, the five Princes were galloping around on their winged horses when they came near the zoo. There, they saw a monkey and an owl sitting atop a tall palm tree. The Princes called to one another, "Let's catch those animals! We'll take them home and keep them as pets!"

Poor Buddhu and Bhutum were unable to escape the Prince's horrible nets. They were carried back to the royal palace and promptly imprisoned in a cage.

After a long day of work, the banished Ranis came home to find their precious sons missing! Since they knew Buddhu and Bhutum would not have run away, the mothers feared the worst for their sons. They clung to each other in sorrow, weeping pitifully.

*   *   *

Buddhu and Bhutum were stunned at what little they could see from inside their cage. The palace was a wondrous place with horses, elephants, soldiers, jewels—so many things they had never witnessed before! They thought to themselves, "How lovely! With so much comfort in the world, why do we play in a palm tree? Why do our mothers live in a ramshackle hut?"

They asked their captors, "Oh, good Princes! Since you have been so kind as to bring us to this heavenly palace, won't you please bring our mothers here as well?"

"Our new pets can speak like human beings!" exclaimed the Princes, adding, "Tell us, monkey and owl, where your mothers live, and we will surely escort them to the palace!"

Answered Bhutum, "My mother is the sweeper at the zoo."

Answered Buddhu, "My mother is a rag-picker by the forest."

The Princes, who did not know about the banished Na-Rani and Choto-Rani, began to laugh uproariously. "As if a human being can give birth to an owl! As if a human being can give birth to a monkey!"

But there was an old soldier who overheard this exchange. He exclaimed, "Your Majesties, there were once two Ranis in this palace who gave birth to such creatures. Indeed, this owl and this monkey are those very same princes!"

"Shame! Shame!" sneered the Princes, kicking the cage in which Buddhu and Bhutum sat. They told the soldier, "Throw these animals out!" With this order, the mean-spirited Princes mounted their horses and rode away into the countryside.

For the first time in their lives, Buddhu and Bhutum realized they were the Raja's sons. Bhutum knew his mother was not a sweeper, Buddhu knew his mother was not a rag-picker. Bhutum said to his brother, "Dada, let's go see our father." Buddhu agreed, "We must find a way to meet him."

*   *   *

The five Ranis were sitting on golden thrones, their feet resting on silver footstools, when a palace maid ran in and informed them, "Rani-Ma, Rani-Ma, there is a beautiful white-sailed ship in the harbor that has silver oars and a diamond studded rudder. Upon it is a milk-rose princess with hair like the monsoon clouds, talking to a golden tia bird."

Hearing about this spectacular princess, the Ranis ran pell-mell to the river bank. Each vied with the other to make the milk-rose maiden her daughter-in-law. But when they reached the harbor. the ship was already in full sail, pulling away. The Ranis held out extraordinary jewels of the finest quality and luster, calling,

> Milk-rose maiden with monsoon hair
> Return to shore for our gifts so rare!

But the Princess ignored the enticements, saying,

> Rubies, diamonds, sapphires may stay with you
> Send your sons, oh mothers, to a country new
> A drum and cymbal market, a leafy fruit tree
> Past three crone-kingdoms to the red-river sea.

Anxious to find out how their sons could marry this lovely princess, the Ranis asked,

> Where is your palace, where is your land?
> How can our brave sons win your hand?

By then, the swift ship had sailed quite far. The bewitching maiden sang out over the waters,

> I'm Kalabati Princess with rain-cloud hair
> Tell your royal sons to search with care
> For drums are magic and pearl-flowers hide
> He who finds them will win this bride.

With these mysterious words, Princess Kalabati disappeared into the horizon, the sails of her ship billowing in the wind.

*   *   *

The Ranis rushed back to the palace, and told their sons about the beautiful princess. When the Raja heard all that had happened, he ordered five swift peacock-shaped ships be constructed to transport his sons to Kalabati's land. He then invited all the people of the kingdom to bless the Princes before their journey.

When Buddhu and Bhutum heard this invitation, they realized it was their chance to meet their royal father. They made their way to the Raja's court. When the guard demanded they identify themselves, Buddhu and Bhutum answered proudly, "I am the Monkey Prince!" and "I am the Owl Prince!"

The two brothers flung the doors of the court open and bounded into the throne room. With one leap, Buddhu landed on the Raja's lap. With one swoop, Bhutum perched upon the Raja's shoulder. They cried in unison, "Baba! Baba!"

The Raja's heart was touched and great tears of joy began rolling down his cheeks. He embraced his long-lost sons. "Oh Buddhu and Bhutum," he said, "you have honored your unjust father!" The happy King left the court with his newly found sons in his arms.

In the meantime, five swift peacock-shaped barges were waiting in the harbor. With grand pomp and ceremony, the Ranis prepared to send their sons in search of Princess Kalabati. Just then, Buddhu and Bhutum arrived at the riverbank with the Raja.

"What are those, Baba?" asked Bhutum.

Answered the Raja, "Why, those are peacock-barges, my son."

"Baba, may we sail in a peacock-barge?" asked Buddhu.

At that, the Ranis began screeching in protest. "Are those animals in the Raja's arms?" they howled. "Shame! Shame! These are the children of the lowly sweeper and rag-picker women!"

The Ranis slapped Bhutum across the face and boxed Buddhu's ears. They then bustled the stunned Raja back to the palace, grumbling all the while.

Poor Buddhu and Bhutum picked themselves up from the dust and declared, "Let us go to the ship-builder and make ourselves a peacock-barge. We will sail after the Princes and see where they are going."

*   *   *

Days passed and nights passed. Buddhu and Bhutum did not return home. Their mothers cried endlessly for their lost sons. One day, they heard that the Princes of the kingdom had set sail in five peacock-barges in search of the mysterious Princess Kalabati. Hearing this only made them cry harder. "Our poor sons will never have a chance to seek the hand of Kalabati."

With tears swimming in their eyes, the two mothers walked down to the river. They took two pieces of dried betel-tree bark and set them floating on the water like two toy boats. They blessed these barges with vermilion for luck, cowrie shells for wealth, green paddy and blades of grass to wish their sons long lives. The Ranis imagined these were peacock barges to carry their sons to Kalabati. They recited,

> Owl and Monkey Princes, each a Rani's son
> Cursed by fate
> before their lives had begun
>
> Five peacock-barges to seek a princess sail
> If our sons could go
> they would win her without fail
>
> Buddhu and Bhutum, return to our sides
> The gods will protect you
> and bless you with brides.

The Ranis set the betel bark ships sailing and went back to their humble shack.

On their way to the ship-builder's shop, Buddhu and Bhutum spotted the two tiny boats floating on the river. The brothers decided that these were good enough transportation for them. Each one boarded their betel bark ship and sailed for Kalabati's kingdom.

And the Princes? In their speedy barges, the five brothers had already reached the country of the three crones. They expected a grand welcoming party at the harbor. Instead, to their surprise, their ships were attacked by ferocious soldiers. The

Princes were taken prisoner. The five arrogant brothers were unceremoniously thrown into sacks and brought before the three old hags. The crones were enormous witches, who promptly swallowed the brothers whole and laid down to sleep.

In the middle of the night, while the crones snored, the brothers talked among themselves from inside the witches' stomachs. They mourned, "We are doomed to remain here forever. Never again will we see our parents."

Suddenly, someone whispered to them from the outside, "Dada, Dada!"

The Princes replied softly, "Yet, brother! Who is there? We are trapped inside the witches' belly."

The instructions came, "Hold on to our tails and we will get you out!"

The Princes did as they were told, and were pulled out through the crones' nostrils. They were amazed to find that their rescuers were none other than Buddhu and Bhutum, the owl and the monkey. As soon as the Princes were free, they jumped on their five peacock-barges and without even a backward glance, sailed swiftly away. No one asked Buddhu and Bhutum how they got there or how they would continue on their journey.

*   *   *

In no time at all, the five Princes reached the menacing and vengeful red river sea. All around them was swirling red water, with no land, people or a kingdom in sight. The Princes could not find their bearings and were soon hopelessly lost.

For seven days and seven nights the five peacock ships tossed and turned in the treacherous currents. Finally, the barges could stand no more and began to break apart. The Princes wailed, "If only Brother Buddhu was here, he would save us! If only Brother Bhutum was here, he would save us!"

Out of nowhere, two small voices piped up, "Yes, brothers, how can we help you?" Buddhu and Bhutum leapt from their betel ships onto the peacock-barges and took charge. "Set your sails to the north," they directed.

Following these instructions, the five Princes soon left the

35

tumultuous red sea behind and found their barges at the mouth of a calm river. As they sailed in, they found the banks shaded by mango trees, heavy with fruits. The Princes ate their fill of luscious mangoes and cooled themselves with sweet river water.

Once sated, the Princes curtly inquired, "Why are these two animals polluting our royal barges? Throw the filthy creatures overboard!"

Buddhu and Bhutum were ruthlessly tossed into the river with their tiny boats flung after them.

The five peacock-barges set sail again. After gliding along peacefully for a few leagues, the brothers spotted a large eddy in the river. The forceful currents of the whirlpool sucked their five ships in. The Princes could do nothing to save themselves, and they sank without a trace.

After some time, the betel bark ships reached the same spot in the river. Feeling something was amiss, Buddhu exclaimed, "Something has happened here! Before we go on, let me dive under the water and investigate."

Bhutum agreed, "Alright, brother, you go. But tie this piece of string to your waist. Tug on it when you want me to pull you up."

Buddhu dove into the river and, to his surprise, found a long tunnel under the water. He went through it with caution and discovered a stately kingdom at the other end. However, there was not a soul in sight, save a hundred-year-old woman who sat embroidering a shawl. As soon as she saw Buddhu, the old woman hurled the shawl on him. In an instant, hundreds of soldiers encircled Buddhu, tied him up tightly and took him to the palace.

Without any explanations, the soldiers threw Buddhu in a dark dungeon. Immediately, several voices cried out, "Dear Brother Buddhu, we are so glad you are here! You must rescue us from this beastly place!"

Buddhu was surrounded by his five ungrateful step-brothers.

The next day, Buddhu sprawled on the floor pretending to be dead. The palace servants who brought food to the prisoners, wrinkled their noses at the dead monkey and took away the carcass. Buddhu was thrown on a garbage heap.

Once everyone had gone, Buddhu sat up and started his secret search for Kalabati. He looked for the beautiful Princess all over the palace and finally found her alone on the terrace, talking to the golden tia bird.

All efforts gone to waste, what a crying shame
With silver oars I traveled the world, not a prince came!

Buddhu noticed the white blossom crafted from snowy pearls adorning the maiden's hair. He quietly picked up the jewel without the Princess being aware of it. The tia bird sang,

Rose-milk Princess, shake off your gloom
Where's your hair-gem, your pearly bloom?

The astonished Princess put her hand to her hair and discovered that the pearl blossom was missing! The tia bird chirped on,

Kalabati maiden, do not fear
Look, dear lady, your love is here!

The Princess turned around to find a small monkey with the precious jewel in his hand. Devastated at the implications, Kalabati crumpled to the floor in a dead swoon.

But the fair Princess had no choice. She had vowed to marry anyone who could cross the kingdom of the three fierce crones, sail through the dangerous red river sea, slip by the sly old woman of shawls, flee from her pitch-dark dungeons, and then steal her hair-jewel. Now, she had to marry this animal. Kalabati gave the garland around her neck to Buddhu as a seal of faithfulness.

Once married, Buddhu requested his wife to free the Princes. Then Buddhu told Kalabati, "Princess, now you must come home with me."

The Princess replied, "Of course, now that I am your wife, I must do as you tell me." She showed a small bejeweled box to her husband and said, "I live in this box. I will stay inside it for you to carry me with ease."

As soon as the Princess entered the box, her pet tia bird crashed a pair of cymbals and banged on a drum. Instantly, a market full of bustling tradespeople and villagers appeared like magic. In the melee of merchandise, the box where the Princess was hiding became lost.

No matter how hard Buddhu tried, he could not identify his wife's box. "This is a crazy problem," thought he. "How do I find a solution?"

Buddhu started to beat on the drum and cymbals at will. When he struck the drum, the marketplace was in full swing; but when he crashed the cymbals, the merchants and the busy scene would vanish into thin air. The monkey prince shut his eyes and kept his music of drum and cymbals roaring.

In a while, the merchants and villagers begged for mercy. They were so tired of appearing and disappearing that they handed over the Princess's box to Buddhu and called an end to the deception.

Buddhu took the box but did not give up the drum and cymbals. He opened the lid, saying,

Come home with me, my Princess bride
From your husband do not hide.

Kalabati came out of the box and said, "Yes, I will go. But I am hungry and must eat. I can only eat those fruits that hang from the leaves of a special tree. Won't you please get some for me?"

Buddhu searched for the tree all over the Princess's land. Finally, he found it in a lonely corner of the palace garden. The tree was strange, even incredible. It was covered with large leaves, and from each leaf hung a different colored fruit. They all looked succulent and tempting.

But when he came near the tree, Buddhu found a large python curled around the trunk. It hissed and spat at him, its split tongue striking out. It was impossible to approach the tree with the serpent on guard.

38

But Buddhu was not one to be easily discouraged. He circled the tree once, pulling the string that was tied to his waist. The sharp string dug into the snake and cut it in two. After getting rid of the python in this way, he climbed up the tree and gathered as many fruits as he could carry.

When Buddhu presented the fruits to Kalabati, she accepted defeat. "I have tried to dissuade you by sending you on perilous missions. But you have come through each with flying colors. I will refuse you no longer. Let us leave for your home."

Buddhu replied, "But before I go, you will have to set my five brothers free and return their peacock-barges. And you must also give me the shawl the old woman was embroidering."

The Princess complied. Then, Buddhu tied the drum and cymbals to his back, draped the shawl over his shoulder and stuck the pearl hair-jewel behind his left ear. While chomping on a fruit from the leafy tree, he tugged on the string around his waist.

Bhutum, who was waiting in his betel bark ship, felt a tug on the string he was holding. Immediately, he pulled it up and was amazed to see not only his brother, but the five other Princes, their five peacock-barges, and a mysterious box.

The five peacock ships hoisted sail toward home. Buddhu leapt upon the deck of one and Bhutum flew up to the mast of another. The other Princes noticed that Buddhu was behaving strangely aboard the ship. From time to time, he would lift the lid of the box he carried and speak in undertones. The five Princes wondered, "Who is the monkey speaking to?"

Late that night, while Buddhu and Bhutum were fast asleep, the five Princes stole the box from Buddhu's sleeping arms. Then with a mighty heave-ho they threw the monkey, his shawl, his drum and cymbals into the water. Bhutum was tossed into the river after his brother.

Upon the peacock-barge, the Princes opened Buddhu's mysterious box. They were astonished and jubilant to find Princess Kalabati there. They asked her brusquely, "Who will be your husband now, Princess?"

Answered Kalabati, "Whoever possesses the magic drum and cymbals."

"Ah, we see!" Princes growled angrily. "Since you refuse to marry us, we will have to lock you up!"

And so, the poor Princess was locked in a dark dungeon for the rest of the journey.

Soon, the five peacock-barges sailed into the river harbor. The entire kingdom, the Raja and the Ranis all gathered at the riverbank to see what the Princes had brought home. A wondrous hush fell over the crowd when they spied the five young men returning with the delicate monsoon-haired milk-rose maiden.

The excited Ranis blessed Kalabati by lighting five oil lamps and blowing into five conch shells. As they welcomed their future daughter-in-law into the palace, they asked, "Princess, who will you marry?"

Answered she, "Whoever possesses the magic drum and cymbals."

In turn, each of the five Ranis asked if their son possessed these objects. And, in turn, each received the same answer: "No." Infuriated, the Ranis threatened, "Then, my wily Princess, we will have to kill you."

Kalabati knew she would have to buy some time if she were to survive. "For the next month, I am engaged in ritual prayers," she explained. "After that, whatever happens, will happen."

The Ranis agreed. They thought, "In this month, perhaps she will change her mind and marry one of our sons!"

*   *   *

Meanwhile, Buddhu and Bhutum's mothers were still mourning their lost children. One day when they went down to the river to bathe, they heard two small voices calling from the river-reeds, "Ma!" "Ma!"

And who do you think they found? Their precious Buddhu and Bhutum had returned home! Ecstatic, they carried their children back to the humble hut.

The next morning, the people of the kingdom saw a startling sight. A grand marketplace had suddenly sprung up where there had once stood the lowly hut of the zoo sweeper and rag-picker. Spices, silks and the finest of merchandise were laid out for trading. And surrounding this market were enormous orchards of trees whose leaves hung heavy with colorful fruit. In the center was a sparkling house guarded by uniformed soldiers. It was a remarkable scene indeed!

Buddhu and Bhutum had created the market by beating upon the drum and cymbals. The soldiers had emerged from the embroidered shawl, and the trees had sprung up overnight from the magic fruits of Kalabati-land.

When news of this miraculous market reached Kalabati's ears, she knew exactly who was responsible. She announced to the Raja, "My ritual prayers are over. You may kill me now, if you want." The Raja was astonished. Why would he want to kill the beautiful maiden? But when Kalabati revealed the Ranis' threat, he realized the evil hearts that beat within his five queens. He learned too of Buddhu and Bhutum's bravery, their mothers' hardships.

With tears in his eyes, the Raja immediately dispatched the royal musicians and palanquin-bearers to escort Na-Rani and Choto-Rani back to the palace. The five wicked Ranis and their sons did not take the news well. They locked themselves up in their palaces and were never heard from again.

The next day, with grand pomp and celebration, Buddhu was married to Princess Kalabati. Bhutum was married to a princess from a neighboring kingdom, Hirabati. The four lived happily in the royal palace with their father and mothers.

*　　*　　*

Late one night, Kalabati and Hirabati woke to find their husbands missing! They searched frantically, but could only find a monkey skin and a heap of owl feathers in a dark corner. The Princess wives thought to themselves, "Are our husbands really humans in disguise?"

Their suspicions were confirmed when they spied two handsome princes chatting in the moonlit garden. They realized that those were indeed their husbands. Promptly, Kalabati and Hirabati burned the feathers and skin.

The brothers ran back, exclaiming, "What have you done?

41

What have you done? A sanyasi had cursed us to remain in monkey and owl forms until our wedding days. Since then, we have been able to escape our animal forms every night to visit the land of the gods. Now that you have burned our animal skins, we will never be able to return to that divine kingdom!"

The wives replied, "Then you must live happily in this earthly kingdom with us!"

The next morning, the kingdom awoke to find two heavenly Princes seated beside the proud Raja. Everyone thanked the gods for such a blessing. The Raja, Na-Rani, Choto-Rani, Prince Buddhu, Prince Bhutum, the Princesses Kalabati and Hirabati began living their days in happiness and joy.

THE PRECIOUS BIRD

There once was a birdcatcher who specialized in catching and selling rare birds. Despite his greatest efforts, he just could not make ends meet. Many a day, the birdcatcher and his wife went hungry. One morning, his wife said, "Husband, do not sell all the birds you catch. Keep a few for us to eat. That way, we will at least be able to fill our bellies."

The birdcatcher agreed to his wife's suggestion. He searched the deepest sections of the forest all day, but did not find a single bird. Finally, on his way home that evening, he caught a beautiful hiremon bird. He went home and handed the bird over to his wife.

But as soon as the birdcatcher's wife laid eyes on the bird, she said, "Oh Ma! What a beautiful little bird! I could not bear to kill it."

Promptly, the hiremon bird spoke. "Dear Aunt, do not take my life," it chirped sweetly. "Take me to the Raja, and he will pay a great price for me."

The birdcatcher and his wife were astounded to hear the hiremon speak. They asked, "But you are such a tiny bird! How much could we possibly get for you?"

Hiremon replied, "Do not worry about that. When you take me to the Raja, just tell him that the bird will set its own price. Trust me, and I will fetch you a good reward."

The next day, the birdcatcher took Hiremon to the royal palace. He said, "I have brought this bird to sell the Raja."

The Raja was enchanted by the pretty bird. He asked, "How much do you want for it?"

Said the birdcatcher, "Rajamoshai, this is a very special bird. You must ask it directly and it will tell you its price."

43

In disbelief, the Raja spoke directly to the hiremon. "So, how much must I pay for you?"

"My price is ten thousand rupees," replied the bird without hesitation. "It may sound like a great deal, but trust me, Sire, I will be of enormous help to you."

Astounded at hearing the hiremon speak in a human voice, the Raja paid the birdcatcher the requested sum. The elated man ran home to his wife. Their life of poverty was over!

* * *

In no time, the Raja became very attached to the hiremon. He would spend all day and night chatting with the bird. He grew so enamored with his new pet that he began to ignore his six Ranis. Hardly did he visit them anymore.

The Ranis became so jealous of the bird that they decided to destroy it. However, no matter how much they tried, they could never get near it. The Raja was always with his precious bird. Eventually, the Ranis found an opportunity. The Raja was going on a hunt, and would be away from the palace for two nights and two days. The Ranis decided that they would have to kill the bird while he was gone. They might never get another chance like this. But who would do the actual deed?

"We will ask the bird to judge who is the ugliest among us," they decided. "Whoever the bird chooses will have the honor of breaking its feathered neck!"

The six Ranis went to the room where the bird was kept. Before they could ask anything, the hiremon began to sing sweetly. So divine was the melody that the Queens could not bring themselves to harm the bird.

The next day, the Ranis blamed each other for the failure of their mission. "We cannot afford to be weak, the Raja will be home soon! We must kill the bird today," they vowed.

Again, they went to Hiremon. Before the bird had a chance to begin singing, the Ranis demanded, "We hear you are a very wise bird. Tell us then, who is the most beautiful among us, and who is the most ugly?"

Clever Hiremon had already guessed the Ranis' evil intent.

He nodded sagely and replied, "Rani-Ma, if I am to give an honest opinion, you have to release me from my cage. I must be able to see all of you from head to foot before I can give my judgment."

Set the Raja's favorite bird free! What if it escapes? The Queens shut all the chamber's doors and windows before they opened the hiremon's cage. But the bird had already surveyed the room and set its escape plan. There was a small drain opening in the far corner of the chamber that was just big enough for it to squeeze through.

Once free from his cage, Hiremon gave his verdict. "Rani-Ma, all of you may be pretty. But, beyond the seven seas and thirteen rivers there lives an exquisite Princess who is more lovely than all of you put together. Even the little toe of her left foot is more beautiful than all of you."

The incensed Queens came after the bird with murder in their eyes. But Hiremon quickly slipped through the drain hole and flew out of the palace. He took shelter in the nearby hut of a kindly woodcutter.

When the Raja returned from his hunt the next day, he was distraught at the loss of his beloved pet. His Ranis claimed ignorance, saying, "How should we know about your little bird? You never allowed us near it!"

The Raja could not stem the flow of tears. So distressed was he that his ministers feared for his health. They declared that anyone who could return the Raja's precious bird would be rewarded ten thousand rupees. When he heard the proclamation, the kindly woodcutter immediately took the hiremon back to its master. Like the birdcatcher before him, the woodcutter too received an enormous reward and lacked nothing thereafter.

Reunited with his pet, the joyous Raja inquired, "Why did you leave me, my dear Hiremon? Don't you like my palace?"

The bird told the Raja all that had happened. Furious, the King banished his six Ranis from the palace. They were never seen again.

But the Raja's curiosity was piqued. He asked Hiremon, "Who is this beauty you spoke about, beyond the seven seas and thirteen rivers? Can you take me to see her?"

The bird replied, "Of course, Maharaj. I can take you to her palace. And if you follow my instructions precisely, you may even have the honor of marrying her."

The King agreed. "Take me to her and I will do as you say."

"We will need a winged horse for our journey," explained Hiremon. "If you can find such a swift animal, we will be able to cross the seven seas and thirteen rivers in no time."

"Let's go to the stables," said the Raja. "Perhaps we can find such a horse there."

The royal stables were filled with the fastest and most powerful horses in the land. The hiremon examined each carefully to see if any of them were actually Pakkhiraj, the winged horse. To the Raja's surprise, the bird passed by all the magnificent animals until it reached the tiniest, weakest looking horse in the stables. Exclaimed Hiremon, "Here it is, Maharaj. This animal is a true Pakkhiraj. This is the horse we need. However, we must feed it the best hay and oats in order to prepare it for the journey."

The Raja made special arrangements for the small horse. It was to be given the best treatment, and receive the most nutritious food. Gradually, the once weak horse grew large and powerful. After six months had passed, Hiremon declared, "Our steed is now ready."

Then the bird told the King, "Ask your jeweler to make us a bag full of silver kernels. We will need them."

With the silver kernels is one hand and the bird upon his shoulder, the Raja was now ready to leave. Hiremon gravely instructed him, "You may touch the horse with your crop only once. He will take us unerringly to our destination. But should you use your crop any more, the horse will immediately stop flying." The bird continued, "On our way back, you must do the same."

The Raja listened to Hiremon intently. He urged his steed only once with his whip and the horse soared to the sky, making fastest speed toward the beautiful Princess's palace. All day, they crossed villages and kingdoms, mountains and deserts. By the evening, the winged horse had crossed seven seas and thirteen rivers. It halted gracefully beside the Princess's palace.

Hiremon told the King, "Maharaj, you must not let anyone see us here. Hide the horse behind the bushes and climb to the top of this large tree." The Raja promptly complied.

The bird took the bag full of silver kernels in its beak and flew inside the palace. He dropped the little seeds as he flew, making a trail from the Princess's quarters to the tree where the King was hiding.

Later that night, the Princess emerged from her bedchamber and saw the silver kernels shining in the moonlight. Curiously, she picked a few up and followed the gleaming trail outside the palace. She stopped at the bottom of the tree, and looked up to see a handsome face high in the branches; the face of love. The Princess smiled radiantly.

The hiremon cried to the King, "Here is your bride, Raja! Carry her to your kingdom."

The King lost no time in lifting the beautiful Princess upon his steed. He touched the winged horse once with his crop and the horse started to fly homeward. However, the King's eagerness to return with his new bride was his undoing. Forgetting Hiremon's admonishment, he struck his horse a second time. Immediately, the wings of the flying horse turned to stone and he dropped from the sky into the forest below.

Hiremon admonished the King furiously "What have you done? Why did you not do as you were told? You may have put us all in danger in this strange and lonely place!"

Nothing could induce the Pakhiraj to move. With the horse and bird, the Raja and the Princess sought shelter in a grassy knoll for the night.

*   *   *

The next day, the countryside was teeming with the hunting party of a greedy and cruel Prince from a nearby kingdom. While chasing a deer into the deepest recesses of the forest, the Prince came upon the Raja and his ravishing companion. So mesmerized was the Prince by the maiden's beauty that he decided to take her for his wife. Without a moment's hesitation, he commanded his soldiers to seize the enchanting Princess and destroy her protector.

The followers did as their Prince ordered. They abducted the Princess but did not take the King's life. He was blinded by the cruel Prince's courtiers and left to roam the forest.

The Prince captured the winged horse along with the Princess and took them both to his palace. He revealed to the beautiful maiden his intentions of marrying her at the earliest opportunity.

The Princess knew she could not dissuade him by argument. So she declared, "I have taken a vow not to marry before my winged horse regains his strength. It will take the animal six months to be well again. The wedding plans will have to be postponed until then."

Finding her resolute, the Prince consented to the delay. The Princess was allowed separate quarters where she could take care of the winged horse in peace. There, the lovely maiden waited for word from the blinded Raja. Although she racked her brains, she could not find a way to escape the clutches of her vicious captor. She realized nothing could be accomplished without Hiremon's help!

*　　*　　*

One day, the Princess announced that she would feed all the birds of the kingdom to bring good luck to her feeble horse. The servants placed tons of bird seeds on the roof of the palace at her request. Every day, hundreds of birds came to feed upon the delicious fruits and grains she put out for them. But although the Princess kept close watch, she did not ever see Hiremon at the feast.

In the meantime, the hiremon was struggling to survive in the dense forest, while taking care of his blinded Raja. For their meals, he collected heavy fruits from the abundant trees. To quench the blind Raja's thirst, Hiremon brought droplets of water in his beak from nearby ponds. For a tiny bird, this was a hard task indeed!

48

Seeing him struggle so, the other birds of the forest told Hiremon about the pious lady in the neighboring palace. Since her arrival, all the birds far and near were no longer worried about their daily meals. All they had to do was to show up at her rooftop for food.

Wise Hiremon thought doubtfully, "Maybe this is not just a devout woman fond of birds. I am sure this is our own Princess!"

As soon as the hiremon flew to the palace, his suspicions were confirmed. He saw the radiant maiden from the land beyond the seven seas and thirteen rivers, surrounded by grateful birds. Hiremon quickly realized she was a prisoner at this palace.

The Princess was jubilant to see the hiremon. They talked for a long time about what had transpired, and the unhappy maiden inquired after the Raja's health. She could not hold back her tears when she heard about the difficulties that the King and Hiremon were experiencing in the forest. Without wasting time, the bird started planning for the Princess's escape. But the first thing to do was to heal the blinded Raja.

"I know of things earthly," said Hiremon, "but not of things magical. Beautiful Princess, how can we restore his sight?"

The Princess thought for a while, then advised, "In the northwest corner of my palace, there grows an enormous tree thick with green leaves. A wise Bangama and Bangamee bird live on the topmost branches of that tree." She recollected gravely, "I have heard that the saliva of these magical creatures can bring back light to the eyes of the sightless."

"Then I must fetch this right away," cried the little hiremon, and started its journey then and there.

For a long day and longer night, the tiny bird flew on. As soon as he reached the palace of the Princess, he found the gigantic tree that was home to the huge Bangama and Bangamee birds. Hiremon recounted all that had happened to his master and his beloved Princess. His human face smiling kindly, the Bangama bird immediately gave Hiremon the cure.

It took Hiremon another day and a night to fly back to the blind king. "Maharaj, I have brought you a remedy for your ailment!" exclaimed the bird.

In an instant, the Raja's sight was completely restored. As soon as he could see, he cried out for his beloved Princess.

Hiremon assured him, "She is a prisoner, but she is alive. Now that you are well, I will go to bring her back." With these words, the small creature flew to the Princess's quarters.

"The Raja's sight is restored, my dear Princess, thanks to you!" Hiremon rejoiced. "Let us continue now on our unfinished journey."

The Princess called to the winged horse, who had already regained his strength. She sat upon the trusty horse with the tiny bird on her arm and flew to where the Raja awaited her in the forest. Soon, all three were on their way to the Raja's land.

With great pomp and ceremony, the Raja married his beloved Princess from beyond the seven seas and thirteen rivers. For their faithful winged horse, a golden stable was built. The Raja and Rani had many beautiful children and ruled happily, with the wise bird Hiremon forever by their side.

THE UNDERWORLD PRINCESS

There once lived a king's son named Arup Kumar and a minister's son named Sarat Kamal who were very good friends. One day, the two young men decided, "We will soon have to assume the duties of the kingdom. Before that time, let us see the world together." They traveled for many days and nights, seeing towns and countryside, villages and jungles. One evening, after traveling for many miles, Arup and Sarat came upon a mountain, and decided to rest there for the night.

Beside the mountain was a still lake, and beside the lake grew an enormous tree with sheltering branches. Sarat said, "Friend, let us climb up that tree and spend the night in safety."

The Prince agreed readily. The young men set their horses to graze and washed their hands and faces in the lake. Then, they climbed to the topmost branches of the tree and fell asleep.

Later that night, a fearful noise awakened the friends on their perch. The ground shook as if the bowels of the earth were erupting. Arup and Sarat opened their eyes to find the mountainside lit with an eerie glow. The brave young men were filled with terror as they watched, in that unearthly light, an enormous python devouring their horses. After finishing its meal, the python began to roam around within the circle of light, flicking its tongue and tail.

The minister's son whispered, "Do not be afraid, dear friend. The light we see is coming from the jewel that usually rests upon the snake's hood. The python has left the stone beneath this very tree while he feeds. Somehow, we must get it."

"Oh my goodness!" exclaimed Prince Arup. "How can we do that?"

Without a word, Sarat Kamal climbed down from the tree

51

and quietly crept to the lakeside. Gathering a handful of moist soil, he threw it upon the jewel, covering its light. Then, he embedded his sword in the mud over the stone and climbed back up to where the Prince was waiting.

As soon as the jewel's light was extinguished the python rushed back to find its stone was covered with mud. Flailing its body about in the dark, the snake fell on the sharp saber and was cut in two.

The two friends waited in the tree, not daring to climb down until morning. With the first rays of the sun, they came down and found the slain body of the python. Then, they picked up the serpent's muddy jewel and went to the lake to wash it off.

As soon as they dipped the stone in the lake, the cool water parted to reveal a marble staircase descending into its depths. Curiously, Arup and Sarat climbed down the steps and soon found themselves in an underground land. Before them was a beautiful mansion, with a blooming flower garden, shady trees, and lovely vines twisting this way and that.

This was an adventure indeed! The young men headed toward the palatial house, expecting the interior to rival the serenity of the garden. But as soon as they walked inside, they were startled by a terrible noise—like thousands of snakes hissing together. Arup exclaimed, "Let us leave at once! We must run away from this place."

Sarat reassured him, "Do not be afraid. As long as we have the snake's jewel, there is nothing to fear."

Hand in hand, the friends made their way over floors covered with the glistening, slithering bodies of snakes. Finally, they entered a room where the walls were lined with serpents of various sizes and colors. The ceiling, floor, even the furniture moved with hundreds and thousands of snakes covering them. It was as if the room was alive! The chamber was brightly lit from the jewels on the snake's heads. In the center of the room, on a bed of coiled serpents, there slept a breathtaking maiden.

In awe, Prince Arup asked, "Who is this beauty asleep amidst such danger?"

Answered his companion, "She is the Princess of the underworld."

Gently, Sarat touched the python jewel to the Princess's forehead. She awoke immediately and queried, "Who are you young men? I am Princess Manimala, a captive in the palace of the Death Python. How did you two come here?"

"Princess, do not be alarmed. We have killed the fearsome python," said the minister's son. "And this Prince is to be your husband."

Right then and there, Manimala and Arup Kumar exchanged garlands and were married. The snakes of the room writhed in fury, but were afraid to attack the young men because they possessed the powerful python jewel.

The days passed blissfully in the serpent world. But after a few months, Sarat became restless. "Dear friend," he said, "we are so happy here, yet we have no news of our home. Your bride has neither been presented to your parents, nor seen your inheritance. I will go home with the news of your wedding and bring back a welcoming party with musicians and palanquins."

Arup agreed. Again, the friends went to the marble stairs and parted the water of the lake with the python jewel. After bidding Sarat farewell, the Prince returned to the underworld with the luminous stone in his hand.

The newlyweds were now alone. Manimala acquainted her husband with the serpent-land, while Arup Kumar regaled her with stories of the world above the lake. Fascinated by his tales, Manimala mused, "Never in my life have I been able to set eyes upon your world. My dearest wish is to see this marvelous place."

But the Prince ignored his bride's desire.

One afternoon, when Arup Kumar was sound asleep, Manimala decided to explore the above-ground world on her own. She quietly took the python jewel from her sleeping husband and crept up the marble staircase. What a glorious place was this! After years of dark imprisonment in the underworld, Manimala was overcome at the beauty of life under the sun. The sparkling water of the lake enticed her the most. She called to the python stone,

Serpent jewel, burn so bright
I am dazzled by this sight
Calm the waters of the lake
For me to bathe in sweet delight.

At her command, the jewel glowed fiercely and the lake closed over the staircase. Clear water shimmered in the golden sunshine as schools of tiny fish swam about freely, white swans floated elegantly among blooming lotus. Manimala set the jewel on the bank and went in to bathe.

That afternoon, it so happened that the Prince from that very kingdom had come to the mountain to hunt. He saw the fair Manimala frolicking in the lake amidst the lotus blossoms, and instantly fell in love. He recklessly ran towards her. Startled by his approach, Manimala snatched up the python jewel and dove underwater. In the blink of an eye, the idyllic scene changed. The swans and lotus were gone and the lake became a dreary reservoir. The disappointed Prince waited helplessly for the gorgeous phantom to return. It took the Prince's courtiers a long time to convince him to abandon his vigil.

But the Prince was not the only one who had spied Manimala that day. An old rag-picker crone, who had been hiding behind a large bush, had also seen the underworld Princess. She had witnessed the Prince rush to meet the mysterious maiden, then lose her.

Meanwhile, back in his palace the enamored Prince could do nothing else but think about the fairy Princess he had seen in the lonely mountainside. He became deeply dejected. Nothing could lift his mood. Afraid for their son's health, the King and Queen declared that anyone who was able to make their son well again would be rewarded with half the kingdom and their daughter's hand in marriage.

No one came to help the Prince. Finally, the old rag-picker came forward, saying sassily, "Rajamoshai, I have the medicine that will make your child well. But what will I do with your kingdom and daughter? If you agree to hand over the rewards to my son, Pecho, I will start my work."

Beside himself with worry, the King consented.

Now, the rag-picker woman was really a witch with magic powers. She gathered together a bale of cotton and a spinning wheel, calling aloud,

Spinning wheel, spin away
Fly off on the wind today
The Prince is ill, and will be still
until his love comes to his aid
Take me to the serpent maid!

At the witch's command, a forceful wind blew in from the north and carried her to the lake which hid Manimala's underground world. And all the while the crone kept spinning.

In the meantime, Manimala was so enchanted with the world above the lake that she ventured out again. When she saw an old woman sitting on the blanks, spinning yards of gauzy silk, she was delighted. "Where have you come from, old woman? Won't you spin a sari for me?" she boldly inquired.

Immediately, the witch spun Manimala a sari of exquisite delicacy. The Princess danced in joy at her first earthly finery. But her face fell when the old weaver demanded payment. "I have nothing but this jewel," explained the dismayed Manimala.

"Then you must give me that," wheedled the crone.

As Manimala extended the python jewel, the old woman grabbed hold of her arms. She flung the poor Princess onto the wind and chanted,

Spinning wheel, spin away
Fly off on the wind today
The Prince is ill, and will be still
until his love does take his hand
Take us to the Prince's land!

In a flash, the witch transported Manimala to the bemused Prince's palace. The moment he cast his eyes upon her, the Prince became well again.

The grateful King and Queen began to plan their son's wedding with the mysterious Princess. After a long period of depression, the kingdom smiled again as its Prince regained his health. But even as the Prince threw off his cloak of misery, Manimala dressed herself in gloom.

After handing over Manimala, the old witch hid the python jewel beneath her rags and whisked it home to her hut. She too started making marriage plans; her son, Pecho was to wed the King's daughter! The problem was that Pecho had not been home for the last seven years. The excited crone sent out messengers to the four corners of the kingdom in search of him.

Finding no other way to stop her impending wedding, Manimala told the Queen, "I have vowed to remain chaste for a year. I cannot break my promise to the gods. After that time, what must happen will happen." The Queen agreed. One year was not long to wait, especially since her son was well again.

In the underworld, without Manimala and the python jewel, Prince Arup was at the mercy of the snakes. The air was heavy with the poisonous breath of serpents; the touch of their cold scales froze his skin. Arup was cast into a dazed stupor. The vicious snakes wrapped themselves around his body in a torturous embrace. Without a hope of escape, the young Prince descended into oblivion.

Soon, Sarat Kamal returned as promised. He reached the lake with royal guardsmen and trumpeteers, palanquins and horses— all to take home his friends, Arup and Manimala. "Dearest friend," he called, "open the lake and show me the way." There was no answer. Days passed and nights passed, but however much the minister's son pleaded, no one came. Realizing something must have gone wrong, he decided to investigate. Sarat left the royal party behind and went to the nearest kingdom to find some answers.

As soon as he entered the city gates, people asked him, "Do you know Pecho? He is to wed our royal Princess. Pecho's mother, the old rag-picker crone, has been looking for him all over the land."

Cleverly, Sarat Kamal replied, "Of course I have seen Pecho. Now remind me, why is he to marry the Princess?"

The people informed him of the melancholic Prince's miraculous recovery. When he heard about the mysterious woman of the lake, Sarat realized all. "Now, remind me again what Pecho looks like?" he asked.

*   *   *

The next day, Sarat Kamal dressed himself true to the people's description. With ashes on his cheeks, wearing tattered clothing, he went to the old rag-picker's home. Hacking and coughing, snorting and laughing, he danced a crazy jig in her courtyard. The crone ran out pell-mell, crying, "Oh my dearest Pecho, oh the jewel of my heart! There you are, my child! You have come home! See what I have collected for you,

> Throne and kingdom for your pleasure
> Silver, gold and lots of treasure
> A Princess like a precious stone
> The python jewel for you to own!"

The rag-picker took out the python jewel from its hiding place and presented it to her "son." True to form, Pecho danced around crazily with the jewel in hand. The crone continued, "Where have you been hiding your handsome face? The Princess has been pining away for you."

The rag-picker woman immediately went to the King's court. "O Rajamoshai! My pretty Pecho has come to claim his reward. Have you ever seen such grace? I only hope your daughter is worthy of such a husband."

What else could the King do but keep his word? The Princess and "Pecho" were wed that day.

In the wedding chamber, Sarat Kamal told his lovely bride all that had transpired. Seeing her husband's true self, the Princess sighed in relief. "But what will happen to poor Manimala?" she asked. "My brother has made her a prisoner."

Sarat whispered to her, "All that I tell you now, you must go and tell Manimala. Also, give this jewel to her." He handed the precious python jewel to his new wife.

*   *   *

Three days passed. On the fourth morning, Manimala declared to the Prince, "My vow is over and now I must go for my purifying bath in the river. Do not send anyone with me. I will only allow your sister and her husband to accompany me."

The Prince paved the road to the river with silk. Sarat, disguised as Pecho, the Princess and Manimala walked to the river. The moment they reached the water, Manimala called to the jewel,

Jewel mine, leaving me, where did you go?

With the hag

Jewel mine, you've returned, where were you so?

In Pecho's rag

Jewel mine, then take me now, down below!

Before her words could end, the waters of the river parted. Manimala, the minister's son and the Princess vanished into its depths. The Prince wailed, "Hai, hai!" The King and Queen cried, "Hai, hai!" The entire kingdom mourned in grief, "Hai, hai, hai!"

The snakes that had clasped Arup Kumar in his death sleep fell away with the return of the python jewel to the underworld. With musicians playing and conches wailing, Arup and Sarat returned to their own kingdom with their new brides.

The serpents of the underworld kingdom all turned into wisps of air and blew away.

TALES OF FAMILY UNITY

TO *MAMA*'S HOUSE

Clap high! Clap low!
To *Mama*'s house we will go
Ma's brother never scolds
Fun and laughter freely flow
Till *Mami* chases with a stick
We'll have no worry, have no woe

TWO BROTHERS

Two brothers are we
Singing Shiva's song in glee
Grannie's away, so we play all day
We are brothers free!

KIRANMALA

There once was a Raja who had a very wise Chief Minister. One fine morning the Raja asked the Minister, "Tell me, are the people of my kingdom happy?"

The Chief Minister replied, "Your Highness, should I speak with caution or without?"

"Answer with honesty, loyal Minister," the Raja assured him.

Thoughtfully, the Chief Minister said, "Long ago, kings would go hunting. In the day they would hunt, but at night, they would disguise themselves as ordinary people and live among their subjects. In this way, they found out about the people's problems and hardships. Your Majesty, those days have long passed."

"Is that so?" the Raja answered. "I will leave tomorrow for the hunt."

In preparation for the Raja's journey, the kingdom became a frenzy of activity. Elaborate howdahs were placed on the royal elephants, the royal horses were dressed in bejeweled saddles and the royal cavalry put on their braided uniforms. The Raja set out the very next day, accompanied by five brigades of soldiers and innumerable courtiers.

During the day, the Raja hunted. At night, he wandered his kingdom in humble disguise, to listen to the voices of his subjects. One day, while traveling past the home of an impoverished subject, the Raja overheard three young women talking.

The eldest sister was saying, "Sisters, if I can marry a palace stable-hand, then I will be able to eat my fill of fried lentils."

The middle sister then said, "Sisters, if I can marry the palace cook, then I will be able to taste the royal menu each day."

The youngest sister remained silent. Her two elder sisters asked,

"Little sister, what do you want for your future?"

The little sister said in a small voice, "Nothing." But the elder sisters would not take no for an answer. After thinking for a long while, she finally replied, "Sisters, if I marry the Raja, then I will be the Rani."

Hearing her words, the two sisters collapsed laughing. They teased, "What grand appetites our baby sister has!"

The next day, the Raja sent three palanquins and twenty-seven guards to escort the young women to the palace. The three sisters arrived clutching each other in fear. With reassurances, the Raja asked, "Tell me, what were you talking about last night?"

The sisters remained quiet. The Raja then said, "If you don't speak the truth, I will make sure that you are punished." The two elder sisters confessed to their wishes. But the youngest sister still did not say a word. "I have heard everything," the Raja declared to the sisters. "Your wishes will come true."

The next day, the eldest sister married the stable-hand, the middle sister married the royal cook, and the Raja himself married the youngest of the sisters. All three women began happily tending their homes.

*   *   *

A few years later, the Rani was expecting a child. For her confinement, the Raja built a birthing-room with golden walls and marble floors that were studded with diamonds. The Rani then said, "It's been so long since I've seen my sisters. We are three flowers of the same womb; if they come, my confinement will be spent in joy."

So the Raja invited his two sisters-in-law to the royal castle. He paved the road from their homes with silk, and lined the path with musicians who played sweetly to welcome them. The two sisters arrived to see the castle buzzing with excitement. Seeing all the attention being paid to their little sister, they were consumed with envy.

But what did the Rani know of such black emotions? She was happy to have her sisters around her. Late that night, while the castle was sleeping, the Rani gave birth. The little boy was soft as downy cotton, as beautiful as a malati flower, and as radiant as sunshine. The two elder sisters quickly put the child in a clay pot, and set him adrift on the dark river that flowed by the castle.

The next day the Raja asked, "Has my child been born?"

The clever sisters showed him a dog wrapped in royal silks and said, "Your wife gave birth a to a puppy last night." The amazed Raja was silent.

The following year, the Rani was expecting her second child. The two sisters were brought to the castle again at her request. On a dark night, the Rani had a second son. Again, the jealous sisters placed the boy in a clay pot and set him adrift on the river. They told the Raja, "This time, your wife has given birth to a kitten." The confused Raja could not understand why fate had cursed him so.

The next year, the Rani gave birth to a daughter. Like her brothers, the baby girl was beautiful and radiant. Her skin was like clay that has been warmed by the sun, her limbs were strong like early branches of a shishu tree, her eyes were bright like the morning star. Her laughter was like a shower of moon-beams. For the third time, the two sisters set the baby adrift on the river.

This time, they showed the Raja a wooden doll and said, "Here is your little girl." The Raja bowed his head in sorrow and walked away.

The people of the kingdom started wondering. "What kind of Rani has our Raja brought to us? Not once, not twice, but three times she has given birth to amazing creatures: a puppy, a kitten and a wooden doll. She cannot be a human being. She must be a witch or a demon!"

The Raja heard the voices of his subjects and realized, "I have brought a curse upon my house by marrying this unknown woman. To bring back good fortune to my kingdom, I must banish her."

After their tearful little sister had gone, the two jealous sisters laughed in glee and returned to their own comfortable homes.

*   *   *

In a remote corner of the kingdom, at the edge of the great forest, there lived a wise and kind Brahman. Every morning, he would travel to the river for his ablutions. One day, while in the water, he noticed a clay pot floating toward him. Hearing an infant's cry, he opened the lid to discover a beautiful baby boy. The Brahman thought, "Surely fortune is smiling on me. I have no wife, but the river has given me a son." The old man gathered the child in his arms and took him home.

The next year, the Brahman saw a similar pot in the river. Opening it up quickly, he saw to his amazement another baby boy. He thought, "Now my son has a brother to play with," and took the second child home.

The Brahman continued to bathe in the bountiful river. One morning, he saw a third clay pot floating on the river's warm currents. He swam toward it, not daring to hope for a third blessing. Upon uncovering the pot, he was filled with joy to find a newly born baby girl as beautiful as a devi. He thought, "Two sons and now a daughter, my family is complete." Joyously, he rushed home.

The jealous aunts had discarded the three royal children, who now filled the home of the kind Brahman with light. The royal palace remained in shadows.

With his three children, the Brahman knew no sadness. Their lives were prosperous. While the kingdom fell into drought and famine, the Brahman's farm lands yielded golden rice paddy; his trees were heavy with luscious mangoes, berries and jackfruit. While other wells went dry, the Brahman's well overflowed with sweet, cool water. The cows in his shed gave bountiful, frothy milk to make the children grow strong.

The Brahman's household shone with the light of three golden moons. Having been alone for so long, his life was now rich and full with the love of his three children. He named his eldest son Arun, after the sun, and his second son Barun, after the god of the flowing river. His daughter he named Kiranmala, a garland of moonbeams.

Days passed and nights passed. Arun, Barun and Kiranmala

grew like the phases of the moon. They bloomed like three fragrant flowers in the Brahman's garden. When Arun, Barun and Kiranmala laughed, the birds of the forest joined in with songs. When they cried, deer rushed out of the woods to soothe them. In no time, the three grew tall and strong. Together, they learned their lessons and kept their home sparkling. They gathered fruits from the trees, vegetables from the lush garden, and each day decorated their home with fragrant blossoms.

One day, the Brahman called his three children to him. Placing a loving hand on their heads, he said, "My darling Arun, Barun and Kiranmala, all of this is yours. I have nothing more I could want from this world. Leaving you to care for each other, I am going to another place." Sadly, the three children said goodbye to their father.

* * *

In the meantime, the kingdom was drowning in sadness. The palace and countryside were dressed in a cloak of misery and gloom. In his lonely home, the Raja realized, "Fortune has frowned on my kingdom. I must live among my people again, to discover the root of this unhappiness." The Raja and his court prepared once again for a royal hunt.

The day they began their journey, the sky burst. Storm, hurricane and torrential rain beat unmercifully upon the travelers. In the confusion, the Raja became separated from his party. To escape the dangers of pitch darkness and a cruel storm, he took shelter in a hollow tree.

The following day, the Raja tried to find his way to his followers. The rain had not only washed out their footprints, but destroyed the dirt paths. Under a scorching sun, the weary Raja searched in vain for another person and some water to drink. Exhausted, hungry and thirsty, he finally saw a house in the distance and went toward it.

Arun, Barun and Kiranmala were amazed at the stranger on their doorstep. Attired from head to foot in golden jewelry, the man looked like no traveler they had ever seen. But upon hearing the stranger call pitifully for a drink, the brothers and sister ran to assist him. Replenished by their sweet water, the Raja asked, "Who are you beautiful children living in this lonely place?"

Arun replied, "Our father was a respected Brahman."

The Raja's eyes filled with tears at the sight of the three radiant children, each as tall and supple as a young debdaru tree. He said, "Your water has nourished me like a heavenly nectar. Dear children, I am the King of this sad realm. I will always remember your kindness." Heaving a sigh, the Raja left.

After the Raja had gone, Kiranmala asked curiously, "Brothers, what does a king have?"

Arun and Barun replied, "All we know is from our books. A king has elephants and horses and palaces."

Playfully, their sister said, "Since we do not have elephants or horses, let's make a palace for ourselves."

Days passed and nights passed. Arun, Barun and Kiranmala were tireless in their work. In the phase of one moon, they built their magnificent palace. They built walls with rosewood from the forest, floors of cool marble from the mountainside, and towers of sandstone from the riverbank. They strung fresh flowers from the ceilings, and filled the palace with the sweet smell of incense and sandalwood. In the vast gardens around the palace, they invited the animals of the forest to live in peace. The windows of the palace were always kept open so that the birds could fill the house with song. So too were the doors kept open to welcome weary travelers.

One day, a sanyasi traveling by the river saw the wondrous palace. He asked aloud,

> Who built these walls   so strong and tall
>   in this lonely land?
> A wise king knows   the walls of knowledge
>   will never fail to stand.

Arun replied,

> Upon the love of siblings

Does our palace stand
We are the Sun, the Flowing River
and Moonbeam Garland.

The sanyasi did not approach the palace. Instead, he stood
where he was and said in a booming voice,

Arun, Barun, Kiranmala
heed my warning well
Your palace walls will crumble
your home an empty shell
unless the golden fruit
falls from the silver tree
Until the pearly waters of the fountain
can flow free
On a diamond branch the golden bird
must sing a blessed tune
The garden path yield rubies red
that shame the blood-red moon
Only then will your palace have
beauty that is true
The magic bird's every song
will shower bliss on you.

Alarmed, Arun, Barun and Kiranmala called out,

Where is such a golden bird?
Such a silver tree?
Where is the shining fountain
with pearly waters free?

Closing his eyes and holding up a hand, the sanyasi replied,

In the East   of North of East
      the Maya Pahar climbs
Its silver trees   yield golden fruits
      from the ancient times
The cool pearls   of the mountain spring

    flow freely even now
The golden bird   trills magic notes
    upon the diamond bough
Cloaked by enchantment, the Maya mountains hide
Valor, truth and wisdom can be your only guide.

With these mysterious words, the sanyasi was gone. The brothers and sister stood silently, contemplating the meaning of the puzzle. After a few moments, Arun vowed, "We must fulfill the prophecy to protect our home."

The next morning, at sunrise, Arun said, "Brother Barun, Sister Kiranmala, you stay here in our palace. I will go to the Maya Pahar." He gave his brother and sister a sword, saying, "If this sword rusts, then you will know that I am no more."

Months went by. Barun and Kiranmala unsheathed the sword every day to assure themselves of their brother's safety. One day, as he removed the sword from its scabbard, Barun's face fell. He whispered, "Dear sister, our brother is no longer on this earth. As the next oldest, it is now my duty to obtain the objects of the prophecy for our home. I must go to the Maya Pahar." He added, "Keep this bow and these arrows. If the bow snaps and the arrows break, then you will know that I have joined our father and brother."

After days of hard travel, Barun arrived at the Maya mountains. The moment his foot touched the base of the mountain, he heard the music of phantoms all around him. Through the Maya mist, he saw figures of apsaras dancing. Voices called to him, "Young Prince, turn back! Look behind you! Hear our call!" The piteous cries broke Barun's resolve to reach his goal. The moment he turned around, he felt his limbs grow heavy.

Arun and Barun, once loving brothers, were now two gray stones of the Maya Pahar.

At home, Kiranmala woke to find the bow snapped, the arrows broken. She realized her brothers were gone.

Kiranmala did not waste her time crying. She cleaned the stables, fed the animals and watered the plants of the garden. Then, she strapped Barun's bow to her back and took Arun's sword in her hand. Dressing in the clothes of a young prince, she headed in the direction of the great Maya Pahar.

Kiranmala ran so quickly through the countryside that villagers mistook her for a shooting star. The very earth beneath her feet turned red, as if it were on fire. Scattered behind her lay day and night, hills and forests, sunshine and rain. Straight and swift as an arrow, she ran on. Storms were put to shame by her intensity, lightning was startled by her speed. In thirteen nights and thirteen days, Kiranmala reached the mountains.

In an instant, Kiranmala was surrounded by demons and phantoms, snakes and scorpions, witches and ghosts. One called, "Little Prince, we will destroy you!" Another yelled, "You are helpless in our power!" The noise around her was deafening. Hands were clutching at her clothes. Someone was pounding a fearful rhythm upon her back,

Thakata-dhakata-dang-dang-dhang
The Prince will die, bang-bang-bang
Bring on the death-drums, sharpen sickle
Cymbals crash, his head bash
Turn his bones and heart to ash
Thakata-dhakata-dang-dang-dhang!

Through the din, the voices of Maya called to her, "Little Prince, look back! Turn around! Come to us!"

Rain and hail poured down on Kiranmala, lightning slashed her path. Thunder crashed around her like a thousand drums. The sky exploded as if the world would split in two.

Yet nothing could sway Kiranmala. She did not feel she had to answer the calls of Maya, because she knew she was not a prince. She was not a boy at all! Although the earth under her feet trembled and the walls of the mountain seemed to melt away, Kiranmala kept her eyes straight ahead. Her hand firmly on the hilt of her sword, she stopped only when she reached her goal.

Before her stood the silver tree with golden fruits. The branches were made of sparkling diamonds, and on a bough a golden tia bird sat singing, quite undisturbed by the clamor of ghostly voices. Seeing Kiranmala, the tia stopped singing and loudly ordered, "Good! Good! You finally came! Come! Come! Don't dawdle. Collect the pearly spring water, gather a branch, scrape the earth from your shoes, take some seeds from the tree, and for goodness sake don't forget to take me! After you are done, go bang on that gong. Look sharp! Let's get going!"

Amazed at the talking golden bird, and not quite able to understand the tia above the ruckus, Kiranmala just stood there. The bird snapped,

Come, my girl
No shilly-shallying
This is no time for
dilly-dallying
Water, branch
earth and seed
With golden bird
make fastest speed!

Kiranmala thought it was best to follow the bird's advice. She quickly collected the items and loudly banged the brass gong that the bird had pointed out. In an instant, the mountain became silent. The demons and phantoms, snakes and scorpions, witches and ghosts vanished. The peace of the Maya Pahar was interrupted only by the song of the cuckoo, the whistle of the doyel bird, and the dancing of peacocks.

The tia then ordered, "Kiranmala, sprinkle the pearly water on the stones!" As she scattered the water, the stones began an awful rumbling and grumbling. Where the droplets fell, hundreds of princes stood up from their stony stupor. They gathered around Kiranmala, their brave rescuer. "A thousand eons of blessings upon you!" they cried.

Arun and Barun embraced her, "We are blessed to have you as a sister!" The golden bird above them started its new song,

Sun and River
Garland and Moon
Your happiness
will begin soon!

*　　*　　*

Upon arriving home, Arun, Barun and Kiranmala tended to their animals, watered their plants, weeded their garden, and otherwise put their palace to rights. They chose a quiet corner of the yard to plant the seeds of the silver tree and a diamond branch. Together, they poured the remaining pearl-water into their courtyard fountain. They scattered the ruby-red earth on the path in front of their doorstep. Then they called to the golden tia, "Rest now, wise bird, in your new home."

By the time Arun, Barun and Kiranmala finished these tasks, the silver tree had reached toward the sky. Its diamond branches spread their fingers, and clusters of golden fruit hung heavy toward the earth. The courtyard fountain bubbled forth with luminous pearls. The red earth they had strewn before the doorstep bore ruby pebbles. The golden bird flew to the newborn tree and began its thousand songs.

As the word spread through the countryside about Arun, Barun and Kiranmala's spectacular garden, villagers came from far and wide. "Aha! Aha!" they cried, "What a wondrous sight! It is as if the very palace of Indra has come down from the heavens!" Soon the tale of their magical garden reached even the ears of the Raja. It became known that the great ruler was eager to visit the fabulous site.

The golden bird advised Arun, Barun and Kiranmala, "You must invite the Raja to come for dinner."

The brothers and sister worried, "But what shall we prepare for the royal feast?"

The tia assured them, "Never you mind. I will prepare the menu." Then, as the brothers and sister readied themselves for the evening's festivities, the tia whispered to Kiranmala, "I must be placed at the Raja's right hand during dinner."

The Raja arrived with eleven courtiers, thirteen guards and twenty-seven horses laden with splendid gifts. As the royal group walked around the palace, they were amazed at its splendors, particularly the incredible garden. In comparison, the royal castle seemed dusty, dark and gloomy.

The Raja wondered, "From where did they get such beautiful things? Are these mere mortals? Hai! Hai! If only they were my children!" To hide the tears in his eyes, he suggested they go in for dinner.

In the dining room, the Raja was amazed at the bountiful food before him: platters of fragrant pulao, mouth-watering kurmas, curried vegetables, cool yogurt, payas and sweetmeats for dessert. The aroma wafted through the room. Yet, as he reached for each item, the Raja realized everything was made of jewels. He exclaimed, "How can I eat this?"

A voice retorted, "Why not? Pulao, payas, curry and kurma— what is wrong with these delicacies?"

The Raja said, "Is this a joke? Emerald kurma, sapphire curry, how can humans eat such things?"

The voice piped up, "And how can humans give birth to a puppy, eh?"

The Raja was startled.

The voice continued, "And how can humans give birth to a kitten, eh?"

The Raja realized it was the golden tia bird that was speaking to him.

The bird continued, "Maharaj, if humans cannot eat such things, how can they give birth to a wooden doll?"

Paling, the Raja exclaimed, "What have I done? What have I done?"

The tia said, "Rajamoshai, do you recognize the truth? These three before you are your own children. Their jealous aunts lied to you and set them afloat on the river."

Shaking all over, the Raja embraced Arun, Barun and Kiranmala. "I have been an unjust ruler. I listened to the voice of fear instead of the voice of truth. I must beg forgiveness from you and your good mother."

The wise bird whispered in Kiranmala's ear, "Your mother lives in a small house at the edge of the forest. Go now to bring her home."

Arun, Barun and Kiranmala went to the edge of the forest to fetch their mother. Seeing her beautiful grown children, the Rani exclaimed, "This must be heaven." The brothers and sister tearfully embraced their mother.

The golden bird began its song,

Sun, River and Moonbeam
Earth's treasure, a mother's dream
From loving arms snatched away
Imprisoned in a pot of clay
They blossomed in a father's care
Three hearts that loved and learned to share
They built a palace tall and strong
Were told it could not stand for long
Freedom, justice they must bring
Within their walls must wisdom sing
Truth and valor showed the way
through Maya Pahar's deadly play
Kiranmala, Moonbeam girl
set brothers free with water's pearl
With mother and with father too
their family love is found anew
Moonbeam garland, River and Sun
your story told, my song is done.

And then what happened? Well, for nine days and nine nights, the people of the kingdom rejoiced at the return of prosperity to their land. The two jealous sisters of the Rani bowed their heads in shame and begged forgiveness.

The Raja and Rani, with their three children, their children's children, and several great-grandchildren, ruled their kingdom with happiness for a long, long time.

THE SEVEN BROTHERS CHAMPAK

There once was a Raja who had seven Ranis. The eldest Rani
was haughty and proud, the second was selfish and greedy.
The third and fourth Ranis were quarrelsome, while the fifth
and sixth were mean and lazy. All were jealous of the youngest
Rani, who was gentle, sweet-natured and the favorite of the
Raja.

To the kingdom's misfortune, none of the Ranis bore any
children. The Raja became increasingly worried. "Who will look
after this plentiful land when I am no more?" he thought.

Then, on the first day of spring, it became known that the
youngest Rani was going to bear a child. The delighted Raja
invited all the people of the kingdom to join him in a sumptu-
ous feast. To each of his subjects, he presented a precious jewel
to announce the impending birth of his heir. Everyone was joyous except the elder Ranis, whose faces turned dark with envy.

The Raja gave the youngest Rani a golden conch shell. "Blow
into this conch when the child is born," he said, "and I will
come to your side."

As soon as the Raja had gone, the elder Ranis dismissed the
royal midwives and declared that they would themselves take
care of their youngest sister. Then, the eldest Rani grabbed the
golden conch and blew into it loudly.

As soon as he heard the wail of the conch, the Raja commanded the royal musicians to begin playing. He gathered his
priests, chief ministers and astrologers and hurried to the youngest
Rani's palace. When he arrived, happy and expectant, the elder
Ranis told him, "Your child has not yet been born." The disappointed Raja returned to his court.

No sooner had he returned than the conch wailed again. Again,

75

he rushed to the youngest Rani's palace with priests and ministers, musicians and astrologers. Again, the elder Ranis told him, "Your child has not arrived."

The third time the Raja heard the wail of the conch shell, he headed for the Rani's quarters alone. When he arrived to find no child, he angrily told the elder Ranis, "If I hear the conch wail once more before my heir is born, I will have you all severely punished."

In the meantime, the youngest Rani had given birth to seven sons and one daughter. The children were like blossoming flowers. They shone like eight bright moons in the youngest Rani's palace.

Weak and exhausted, the youngest Rani asked, "Dear sisters, I would like to see my children." The wicked elder Ranis laughed scornfully. "What children?" they exclaimed. "You have given birth to seven mice and a scorpion!" Upon hearing this, the youngest Rani fainted dead away.

The elder Ranis secretly put the children into eight clay pots and buried them in the palace garbage dump. Only when they returned did they blow into the golden conch. The Raja arrived once again with his courtiers. This time, the jealous Ranis showed the Raja seven mice and a scorpion, saying, "Here are your precious heirs."

Frightened at the ill omen, the Raja quickly banished his favorite wife from the palace. The six elder Ranis danced in glee and the sound of their ankle-bells rang throughout the kingdom.

Meanwhile, the poor banished Rani wandered under the scorching sun as a rag-picker. All the rivers of the kingdom dried up at her misfortune, and even the stones of the earth wept at her sorrow.

In this way, the days went on. There was no peace in the Raja's kingdom, no joy in his heart. All the flowers in the royal garden withered away, and the priests worried that there were no fresh blossoms to offer the gods. The Raja fretted that this did not bode well for his unfortunate kingdom.

When all seemed hopeless, the royal gardener came and told the Raja, "Although your garden has died, there is a tree growing tall beside the garbage heap. There, seven beautiful champak blossoms and one delicate parul flower bloom. If you wish, I can pick these buds for the temple offerings." The Raja readily agreed.

It seemed like a perfect plan. However, when the gardener approached the flowering tree, something quite unforeseen occurred. The fragrant parul blossom called out, "Awake, oh seven brothers champak!" The champak flowers lifted their faces and asked, "Why do you call us, little sister?" Parul replied, "The royal gardener has come, will we let him pluck us from our tree?"

The champaks spoke in unison,

Brothers and sister
climb away higher
We'll only come down
for the Raja, our sire.

and all the blossoms hurried to the topmost branches of the tree.

The frightened gardener threw down his basket and ran pell-mell to the royal court, where he related to the ruler all that had happened. Amazed, the Raja wasted no time in heading for the magical tree.

Seeing the Raja, the parul blossom trilled, "Oh, seven brothers champak, awake! Awake!" The champak flowers asked, "Why do you call us, little sister Parul?" Answered Parul, "The Raja himself has come, will we let him pluck us from our tree?"

The champak and parul blossoms hid among the tree's glossy leaves, calling,

Brothers and sister
we won't be seen
We'll only come down
for the Raja's first queen.

The Raja immediately sent for his eldest Rani. However, she too failed to coax the magical flowers to the ground. In succession, the flowers called for each of the six elder Ranis. Yet no one was able to pick the champak and parul flowers from the tree.

The frustrated Raja could not fathom what else to do. He sat down on the ground, his head in his hands. From high above, the blossoms called to him,

We will not come down
for your queens so grand
We can only be touched
by your rag-picker's hand.

Upon hearing this, the Raja sent hundreds of messengers to search the land for the lowly rag-picker. When they brought back a woman dressed in filthy rags, her feet bare and face covered with dust, even the Raja did not recognize the banished Rani. However, as soon as she approached the tree, the champak and parul blossoms showered down all around her.

Seven dazzling Princes and a breathtaking Princess rose up from the flowers and embraced the woman. Their voices chimed in unison, "Ma, Ma, we've found you at last."

The evil deed of the six jealous Queens became clear to the entire kingdom. Trembling in fear, the wicked Ranis ran away, and were never heard from again. The seven champak brothers and parul Princess returned to the palace with the Raja and Rani. For seven days and seven nights, the people of the kingdom celebrated the return of prosperity and joy to their land.

THE PERFECT MAN

Many years ago, there was a Raja. The Raja's greatest sorrow was that he did not have any children. One day, a holy man came before the king and said, "Your Majesty, I will give you a magic root that will bring you children. Once the Rani eats this root, she will bear you twin sons. But, there is one condition. You must give me one of your children in payment for this boon."

Although the condition the holy man proposed was a bitter one, the Raja could not refuse. Without a single heir, who would look after his kingdom and inherit his fabulous riches when he was gone? He gratefully accepted the root.

Soon, the Queen gave birth to identical twin Princes. One year, two years, five years passed, and still the holy man did not come to claim one of the boys. The Raja and Rani assumed, "The holy man must have passed away. Our sons will be with us forever."

The twin Princes grew more handsome and strong day by day. They learned to ride horses, shoot bows and arrows, and practice the art of politics. They were educated by all the finest teachers of the land.

In the Princes' sixteenth year, however, the holy man suddenly appeared in the royal court and demanded his payment. The Raja and Rani were heart-broken. They had never imagined that the holy man was still alive! How could they part with one of their beloved sons?

But it had to be done! The holy man was relentless. The Raja and Rani knew that he had the power to take away not only one son, but turn themselves, their other son, why, their entire kingdom to ashes. But which Prince to sacrifice? The brothers were inseparable, and equally beloved by the parents. The kingdom was thrown into a dismal turmoil.

When the Princes heard their parents' dilemma, each began to say, "I want to go," "I am going."

The younger Prince said to his brother, "Even if by a few seconds, you are the eldest and our father's heir. You must stay and serve the kingdom. I will accompany the holy man."

Said the brother, "If I am the elder, it is your duty to listen to me. Keep our parents company while I go with the holy man."

After shedding many tears, the Raja and Rani finally agreed to let the elder son fulfill their long ago promise.

Before he left, the elder Prince planted a small tree in the inner courtyard of the palace. Gathering his parents and brother around him he said, "This tree is my soul. As long as its leaves are green, you'll know that I am well. But if any part of it turns brown, you will now that I am in trouble. If the entire tree should dry up, I am no more." He then embraced his brother, respectfully touched his parents' feet, and left.

As he traveled with the holy man, the Prince passed by a mother dog with two pups at the edge of a forest. He smiled at the animals, and heard one of the puppies cry out, "How noble the young man is! Ma, I want to go with him." The mother dog replied, "Go, my little one." The Prince happily picked up the tiny animal and continued on his way.

In a little while, the Prince spotted a hawk with two small babies under her wing. One of the little birds chirped, "Ma, I want to go with that noble man." The mother hawk agreed, "Go, my little one." The young hawk flew straight to his master's outstretched arm. Delighted with his two companions, the Prince followed the holy man.

After a long walk, they reached the holy man's abode, a leafy hut far away from civilization. The sanyasi told the Prince, "You will live with me in this cottage. Your main task will be to gather flowers for my daily offerings. There are plenty of fruits for you to eat and cool water to quench your thirst. You may go anywhere you like. But," he commanded, "you must never enter the north section of this forest."

In a few days, the Prince became familiar with his new surroundings. In the morning, he would collect flowers for the sanyasi. After completing his morning worship, the holy man would disappear for the rest of the day and the Prince was left alone to explore the forest at will. He played with the puppy, watched the hawk soar, and ran with the wild deer of the forest.

One day, while chasing after a beautiful deer, the Prince came to the north side of the forest. The deer ran into a magnificent house and he followed it in. Once inside, he could no longer find the animal; instead, he came upon a gorgeous young woman sitting with a pasha board.

The woman welcomed him. "I am so pleased you have come! I hardly ever have visitors. Won't you play a game of pasha with me?"

Mesmerized by her beauty, the Prince agreed.

For the first game, they wagered the hawk. If the Prince lost, he would forfeit the bird, while the woman would give him another hawk if she was defeated. As she rolled the dice in her hand, the lady whispered,

Pasha's magic dice
Roll in my name
Bring your mistress home a hawk
Win me this game.

In the blink of an eye, the Prince lost. Immediately, the mysterious beauty took his hawk and imprisoned the creature in a dark hole in the courtyard.

Wanting to win back his hawk, the Prince requested, "Let's play another hand. This time, I wager my puppy. But if you lose you must return my bird to me."

The woman agreed. Again she called to the dice,

Pasha's magic dice
Roll in my name
Bring your mistress home a dog
Win me this game.

81

And the Prince lost again. To his sorrow, the puppy joined the hawk in the courtyard prison.

For the third round, the Prince wagered his own self. For the third time, the beautiful woman sang,

Pasha's magic dice
Roll in my name
Bring me the sweet Prince
Win me this game.

The woman laughed in glee as she defeated the Prince. She threw him in a dungeon underneath her house.

Actually, the mystery woman was not a human being at all! She was a rakshashi in disguise. Although she drooled with greed at the Prince's tender flesh, she had finished her day's meals already. So she planed to feast upon the Prince and his animals the next morning.

*   *   *

In the meantime, the younger Prince had been checking on his brother's plant every day. Until now, the leaves had been abundant and green. On this morn, the younger Prince woke to find his brother's plant brittle and brown. A panic set about the kingdom. The Raja and Rani realized that their eldest son was in some kind of trouble.

The younger Prince calmed his parents, promising, "Ma and Baba, I will go to find my brother." He too planted a supple tree in the courtyard, explaining, "My welfare is assured as long as this tree is alive. If the leaves should brown and fall, I am unwell, and if the tree should die, so have I."

The younger Prince then mounted the fastest steed in the royal stable and galloped toward the forest.

On the way, he found the same mother dog with her remaining puppy. Since the two Princes were identical, the little puppy said, "You took my brother, Sir, now you must take me."

The Prince realized his brother must have passed this way.

Happily, he lifted the puppy onto the horse and rode on.

Soon, he came upon the mother hawk and her young one. Spying the Prince, the baby hawk exclaimed, "Last time you took my brother, now you must take me."

The young Prince was joyous to realize that he was following his brother's tracks. With the hawk upon his arm and the puppy before him, he continued determinedly.

It was not long before he came upon the holy man's solitary hut. But alas! it stood empty. Neither his brother nor the holy man were in sight.

Freeing his horse to graze, the younger Prince waited inside with the hawk and puppy for company.

After the last rays of the sun had vanished from the sky, the holy man returned. Seeing the young Prince he said, "I am glad you have come. I had warned your brother not to stray to the north of the forest. However, he did not heed my words." He continued ominously, "You see, a ferocious rakshashi lives there who has no doubt captured your brother. Maybe she has even eaten him up by now."

Immediately, the younger Prince leapt upon his horse and hastened to the north side of the forest. He too spotted the comely deer and followed it to the astounding mansion in the woods. Upon entering the house, he lost sight of the deer, but found the beautiful maiden with her pasha board.

The younger Prince thought, "This must be the vicious rakshashi into whose clutches my brother has fallen."

The handsome woman asked, "Since you have come so far, you must play a game of pasha with me."

The Prince readily agreed to the game, wagering his bird. Like before, the lovely lady recited,

Pasha's magic dice
Roll in my name
Do not let your mistress fail
Win me this game.

As she was about to throw down the dice, the younger Prince stopped her. "Wait a minute," he said. "Since I am your guest, don't you think I should roll first?" The rakshashi could not refuse his argument. The Prince picked up the small ivory cubes in his hand. Guessing that the rakshashi might be cheating, he cleverly substituted her dice with his own. He blew in his fist and murmured,

> Twin dice, black and white
> Truest in the land
> Join my bird with brother lost
> Two fates in one hand.

The beautiful woman's eyes widened to see the young Prince win! But she could hardly do anything but comply when he demanded, "You have lost the game. Bring me a bird exactly like mine."

The stake for the next game was the puppy. The Prince cried,

> Twin dice, black and white
> Truest in the land
> Join my pup with brother lost
> Two fates in one hand.

He won again, and insisted, "Now you must bring me a dog exactly like this one."

The beautiful woman was forced to free the little dog from its prison. Jubilant to be reunited with their brothers, the four animals danced around the Prince merrily.

But the young Prince still had another hand to play. This time, he played with utmost care, chanting,

> Twin dice, black and white
> Truest in the land
> Bring me back my brother lost
> Two fates in one hand.

He won again. His beautiful opponent protested, "Where will I find a Prince just like you?" The younger Prince pressed on relentlessly. In the end, the defeated rakshashi brought out the elder Prince. Reunited, the two Princes felt that their half-selves were now completed into a whole.

The two brothers jointly turned upon the rakshashi to wreak vengeance. Fearing for her life, she bargained, "If you do not kill me, I will reveal a secret that will save your life."

The Princes urged, "Tell us your secret."

The rakshashi addressed the elder Prince, "The holy man you serve is not a man of god at all. He is an evil magician who has been trying for a long time to create the perfect man. For his spell to work, he needs the souls of seven young Princes." She continued her gory tale, "Six young men have lost their lives. You are the seventh. He will kill you in two days time, on the night of the next new moon."

Hearing the rakshashi's story, the elder Prince shook his head sadly. "I cannot run away from the magician. I have given my word to serve him."

The rakshashi elaborated, "On that dark night, the magician will ask you to bow before his altar. When you do, he will chop off your head. You must not allow this to happen."

The brothers bid farewell to the rakshashi and came back to the hut. For the next two days, they gathered flowers for the magician and tended to his chores.

As the rakshashi had predicted, on the evening of the new moon, the magician took both Princes to an altar in the woods and asked the elder to bow low. Before he could obey, the younger Prince piped up, "My brother is the son of a king and has never bowed before anyone. He does not know how to do so. Could you please demonstrate?"

Not suspecting anything, the magician bowed low. The younger Prince promptly took a sword and killed him.

With the death of the magician, the six sacrificed Princes came to life again. They thanked the twin brothers profusely before heading off to their respective kingdoms. The brothers, with their two puppies and hawks, returned triumphantly to their palace, never to be separated again.

In the inner courtyard, their soul-trees shimmered vibrantly in the sunshine.

TALES OF CUNNING AND
COMMON WISDOM

THE TOADS' REVENGE

In the weaver's hut, down the street, the toads did make a home
Their tadpole-son, a life begun, did play and sing and roam

The weaver's boy awoke one morn, some evil thoughts in mind
With bamboo stick, he did lick the tadpole's behind

There was a mighty general with smarts and warts so grand
He sent a whooping war-cry throughout the toad-land

From every nook and corner, from every field and stream
Fourteen thousand frogs arrived, their shields and swords agleam

From Hoogly and its neighborhood, no lack of soldiers there
A few brigades of Sepoys came to settle the affair

With loom and spinning wheels, the weavers tried to run
On the path, a vicious toad blocked them with a gun

With loom and spinning wheels, up a tree they race
But there was a froggie there who slapped them on the face

With loom and spinning wheels, they tried a different trick
But on the ground a toad did wait to give them a swift kick

The errant lad fell to his knees from the frog attack
Fourteen thousand toads climbed up on weaver-son's back

Spare our son his cruel ways, the weaver cried in plea
The toads' revenge was called to end in amphibian victory!

TUNTUNI AND THE BARBER

The little bird Tuntuni was dancing in the eggplant garden on a bright, sunny day when a spiky thorn from one of the branches pierced his tiny foot. "O-Ma'go, Ore-Baba, Oof!" he cried, halting his happy jig in midstep. For the rest of the day, Tuntuni limped around, his cheery song silenced by the throbbing pain.

Seeing him suffer, the people of the village advised, "Brother Tuntuni, go to the royal barber and have him remove the thorn!"

Tuntuni hobbled straight to the barber. "Brother Barber, Brother Barber," he asked, "will you please remove this thorn?"

The barber took one look at Tuntuni and turned up his nose. "What nonsense! How can I, who shaves the royal whiskers off the Raja's cheek, touch your foot? Be off, be off!"

Furious, Tuntuni replied, "We'll see who's too grand to help me!"

Tuntuni limped to the royal palace. "Rajamoshai, Rajamoshai," he fumed, "your barber has refused to remove a thorn from my foot! You must punish him immediately!"

The Raja's laugh rumbled deep from his belly. "Ho-ho," he guffawed at the little bird's outrage, and did nothing to help.

Filled with anger, Tuntuni went straight to the palace mouse. The mouse welcomed him,

Brother Tuni
if you please
Come right in
Be at ease
The rice is warm
Pull up a chair
All I have
is yours to share.

"I'll share your rice," answered Tuntuni, "if only you'll do something for me. You must go and bite the Raja on his fat belly!"

"Heyi-Baba! How can I bite the royal tummy?" exclaimed the mouse. "No, no, I can't do that!"

Tuntuni's next stop was the royal cat. "Brother Cat, Brother Cat, are you at home?" he called.

The cat welcomed him,

Brother Tuni
if you please
Come right in
Be at ease
The rice is warm
Pull up a chair
All I have
is yours to share.

"I'll have some rice," said Tuntuni, "only if you catch the mouse for me."

The cat yawned lazily, "Oof! It's time for my nap. I can't chase after a mouse now."

Tuntuni scolded him severely, and went to visit the bamboo stick. "Brother, Brother, are you at home?" he called.

The bamboo stick welcomed him,

Brother Tuni
if you please
Come right in
Be at ease
The rice is warm
Pull up a chair
All I have
is yours to share.

"I'll eat with you," answered Tuntuni, "but first you must beat the cat."

"What has the cat done to me," asked the bamboo stick,

"that I should go and beat him?"

Next, Tuntuni called on the fire. "Brother Fire, Brother Fire, are you at home?"

The fire welcomed him,

Brother Tuni
if you please
Come right in
Be at ease
The rice is warm
Pull up a chair
All I have
is yours to share.

"I'll accept your hospitality," said Tuntuni, "only after you turn the bamboo stick to ashes."

"I've had a very busy day," grumbled the fire, "I can't burn a thing more."

Seething with rage, Tuntuni went to the sea. "Brother Sea, Brother Sea, are you at home?"

The sea welcomed him,

Brother Tuni
if you please
Come right in
Be at ease
The rice is warm
Pull up a chair
All I have
is yours to share.

"I'll be your guest, Brother Sea, if you will drown the fire for me," bargained Tuntuni.

"Drown the fire, and risk drying up?" exclaimed the sea. "Do you take me for a fool?"

By this time, Tuntuni's foot had swollen painfully, which made him rather irritable. He went to the mighty elephant. "Oh, Brother Elephant," he yelled, "will you help me?"

Like all the others, the elephant welcomed him,

Brother Tuni
if you please
Come right in
Be at ease
The rice is warm
Pull up a chair
All I have
is yours to share.

Without bothering with pleasantries, Tuntuni snapped, "Brother Elephant, go and drink up the sea for me."

"I couldn't possibly," said the elephant primly. "If I drink the entire sea, I will explode."

"Explode, my foot," grumbled Tuntuni, and limped off to sit by the marsh. His last hope was the tiny mosquito. "Mosquito Brother, are you home?" he called rather helplessly.

The mosquito hummed in welcome,

Brother Tuni
if you please
Come right in
Be at ease
The rice is warm
Pull up a chair
All I have
is yours to share.

"You seem so generous," Tuntuni sighed, "but will you sting the mighty elephant for me?"

"What a simple request, Brother Tuni, what else is a mosquito for?" he answered quickly.

Within minutes, the tiny mosquito called to all his relatives and friends. Like a gathering storm cloud, millions of mosquitoes rose to darken the sky. Their awful buzzing was a sound more deafening than thunder; the flapping of their wings created a fearful hurricane. They swooped down together upon the elephant.

Then . . .

The elephant cried, "I'll drink the sea!"
The sea rushed, "I'll douse the fire!"
The fire flamed, "I'll burn the stick!"
The stick thumped, "I'll beat the cat!"
The cat yelped, "I'll catch the mouse!"
The mouse squealed, "I'll bite the belly!"
And the Raja ordered, "Off with the barber's head!"

Trembling, the barber fell to his knees. "Forgive me, Brother Tuni, please let me take out the thorn!"

Once the thorn was out, Tuntuni's foot healed quickly and he began to dance again. His songs filled the village, "Tun-tun-a, tun-tun! Tun-tun-a, tun-tun! Tunur, tunur, tun, tun, tun!"

And so it was.

THE FOXY TEACHER

The crocodile and the fox were great enemies. Each would try to trick the other in a constant battle of one-upmanship. But no matter how hard the crocodile tried, the fox was always the winner.

The crocodile thought to himself, "That wily fox always beats me because he is educated. I am a poor illiterate creature of the river—no wonder I lose every time."

For a long while that day, the crocodile snoozed on the banks of the river and considered every possible way of defeating the sly fox. Finally, he sighed, "I have no hope of winning over someone who knows all his letters and numbers. But I will not give up. If my children were educated, they could beat the fox."

The crocodile decided to send his seven sons to be educated. Of course, the only school in the forest was run by the fox! So, the next morning, he dressed his seven children in their finest clothes and took them to the fox's burrow. "Master Fox, Master Fox, are you in?" he called.

The fox, who was at that time munching on some river crabs, responded suspiciously, "What, Brother Crocodile, what's on your mind?"

The crocodile said politely, "Brother Fox, here are my seven sons for you to teach. How will they earn a living if they remain illiterate?"

"Oh, is that all?" queried the fox, popping his head out of his home. "In just seven days, I will make seven geniuses of your stupid sons."

Quite pleased with his decision, the crocodile left his youngsters with the teacher and went back to his favorite spot on the riverbank. "This time I have really outwitted that sneaky fox!" he laughed to himself.

As soon as his foe had left, the fox took one of the crocodile offsprings aside, instructing,

A, B, C, D,
A crocodile lunch for me!

and promptly ate the pupil.

The next day the crocodile came to see how his sons were progressing.

"Famously!" assured Master Fox. "They have already learned much." He went into his burrow and held up the young crocodiles one at a time for their father to see. After holding up five, the fox picked up the sixth student twice. Convinced that he had seen all seven of his children in good health, the crocodile returned home.

The lesson for that day was numbers. The fox took one of his pupils aside, reciting,

One, two, three, four
You're for dinner, five in store!

As before, the second student was swallowed up quickly by his teacher.

Again, the crocodile came to visit his studious children. This time the fox presented the five students one by one, showing the last one three times. Elated at how well his plan was going, the crocodile left.

The fox ate up another of the scholars. And so the days went by, with the fox eating up his pupils and fooling their dim-witted parent.

When only one of the pups was left, the fox displayed it to the crocodile seven times. Then, after the parental visit, the fox ate up the last student.

The next day was the end of the term. However, there were no pupils left! The fox's wife worried, "What are we to do now? If the crocodile finds out what you have done, he will surely eat us!"

95

The fox replied confidently, "Do not distress yourself. That simple dolt will never find us. Let us go to the dense forest on the other side of the river." And so they left.

When the crocodile came to collect his seven geniuses, he found no one home at the master's burrow. "Oh Brother Fox, where are you? I have come for my sons' graduation!" called the crocodile. When he received no response, he decided to investigate. No sooner did he stick his head in the burrow, he discovered tell-tale signs of his children's fate.

Enraged beyond measure, the crocodile searched for the fox high and low. Finally, he returned to the river where he saw the fox and his wife hastily paddling across. As you know, there is no one swifter under water than a crocodile. So, it took him very little time to catch up to the foxes.

Although the fox's wife had already reached the other shore, the crocodile was able to grab hold of the wily master's hindleg. Unable to free himself, the clever fox cried out, "Wife, wife, see what has happened! Something under the water has caught hold of my walking stick. Ah, well, I guess I will lose my favorite cane!"

Upon hearing this, the crocodile thought, "Oh, no! Instead of his leg, I have seized the fox's cane!" As soon as the crocodile let go, the fox bounded in one leap onto the bank. Once on dry land, it was impossible to catch the fleet couple.

After that, the crocodile continued to hunt for the fox. However, he was never able to come close to the cunning teacher. So, the crocodile devised another plan.

One day, the crocodile turned upside down on the river bank and pretended to be dead. When the foxes came to the water side to feast on turtle eggs, they found the prone body. The fox's wife exclaimed, "Finally, the crocodile is dead. Let's eat him."

Familiar with the crocodile's tricks, the fox cautioned, "Wait a minute." He went a bit closer to the body, saying loudly, "Oh no! This crocodile isn't completely dead. If he was fully dead, the tail would waggle and the ears would wiggle."

Immediately, the crocodile began to swish its tail and move its ears. The foxes laughed aloud and ran away.

After this plan had also failed, the crocodile became more determined than ever to catch his foe. He knew that the fox went to the same place in the river every morning to drink. So the crocodile hid himself under the currents at that particular spot.

When the fox arrived, he noticed that there was something wrong. Usually the river was full of fish, but today, the still waters were entirely empty. "Something must have scared the fish away," the fox deduced. "The crocodile must be lying under the water."

The fox called to his wife, "Let's move to another part of the river. The water here is too clear. We need muddy water to drink." Immediately, the crocodile began swirling up the soil from the river bed, making the water murky. Guffawing loudly, the foxes ran from the scene.

So the days went by. The crocodile kept trying to trick the fox, and the fox kept outsmarting the crocodile.

THE OLD WOMAN AND THE FOX

There once was an old woman who was so old that she had outlived all her relatives. She lived by herself at the edge of a village with her two beloved dogs, Ranga and Bhanga. The only family the old woman had left was her great-granddaughter, who was all grown-up, married, and lived in another village far away from the old woman.

One day, the old woman decided she would go visit her great-granddaughter. She instructed her dogs, "You stay here; make sure you don't wander away from home while I am gone!" Ranga and Bhanga obeyed faithfully.

The old lady was making her way out of the village, tottering along on a bamboo walking-stick, when she met a fox. Wagging his long whiskers, the fox declared, "Hey, old woman, I'm going to eat you!"

"Wait," the old woman begged. "If you eat me now, all you'll get is a mouthful of skin and bones. I am on my way to visit my great-granddaughter, who will feed me delicious food and make me nicely plump. Why don't you wait until I return from my trip?"

The fox agreed, "Okay. Go fatten up, and then I'll eat you."

The old woman continued on her journey. In a little while, she was spotted by a tiger, who exclaimed, "Hey, old woman, I'm going to eat you!"

"You don't want to eat me now," the old woman admonished. "Wait until I return from my great-granddaughter's house. Then I will be nice and fat."

The tiger nodded, "Okay. I'll catch you on your way home."

The old woman went a few more paces, leaning heavily on her walking-stick. Suddenly, a bear leaped out of the forest, crying, "Hey, old woman, I'm going to eat you!"

As before, the old woman asked, "Why would you want to eat me now? Wait until I come back from my great-granddaughter's village."

The bear agreed, "Okay. I'll wait until you put some meat on your old bones."

Finally, the old woman reached her great-granddaughter's house. There, she became so fat eating yogurt and cream that she was almost bursting. She asked her great-granddaughter, "Dearest, how will I go home now? The bear, tiger and fox are waiting expectantly to eat me. What will I do?"

Her great-granddaughter replied, "Don't fear, Granny. I will put you in this hollowed-out gourd, and no one will be able to tell you are inside. That way, you will be able to go home safely."

With these words, the great-granddaughter put the old woman in a giant gourd shell, along with a bowlful of puffed rice and tamarind to sustain her on her long journey home. Then, she gave the gourd a mighty push and sent it rolling down the path.

As the gourd rolled along, the old woman sang,

Rolling gourd, rolling gourd
Old woman's gone
Puffed rice and tamarind
Keep rolling on.

A little while down the road, the bear was lying in wait for the old woman. He stopped the giant gourd shell, examining it carefully, but found that it was neither the old woman nor something edible. When he heard the gourd saying that the old woman had already gone, he decided to wait no longer, and sent it rolling down the path.

A bit later, the tiger spotted a large gourd tumbling down the road. He stopped it, looking it over carefully. He was surprised to hear the gourd reciting,

Rolling gourd, rolling gourd

Old woman's gone
Puffed rice and tamarind
Keep rolling on.

"That sly old woman evaded me!" the tiger realized. "Oh well, no point waiting any longer." He too gave the gourd a good push and sent it on its way.

The old woman rolled along in her comfortable gourd, all the while munching on the snacks her great-granddaughter had given her. She merrily continued singing,

Rolling gourd, rolling gourd
Old woman's gone
Puffed rice and tamarind
Keep rolling on.

In the meantime, the clever fox had been waiting patiently for the old woman to return. He spied the gourd, and soon heard the song. Waggling his whiskers, he thought, "Impossible! A gourd can't talk! I have to see what's inside!" He gave a swift kick and broke open the giant shell. Out tumbled the old woman!

"Hey, old woman!" cried the fox, his eyes glistening in greed. "This time you can't escape! I'm going to eat you!"

"Of course," agreed the old woman, "that's why I'm here! But if I may, I'd like to sing you a song before you eat me."

The fox thought over her offer. "Okay," he finally said, "I don't mind a little music before dinner. I don't sing too badly myself; maybe I can join in."

The old woman gave a satisfied smile, saying, "Let's sit on top of that hillock and make sweet music." And so she sang, "Ranga and Bhanga, come to me. Come, come, quickly!"

Within moments, two enormous dogs were bounding down the path toward the old woman and the fox. The fox took one look at their vicious teeth and ran for his life. Laughing heartily, the roly-poly old woman returned home with her beloved dogs.

THE TIGER-EATING FOX CUBS

There was once a fox and his wife who had three cubs. The family's one unhappiness was that they did not have a home in the forest. The mother fox worried, "With the rainy season coming, how will we keep our cubs dry and safe?"

The parents searched high and low, and finally found a nice, dry cave on the side of a hill. They decided to make it their new home.

As she entered the cavern, the mother fox exclaimed, "Oh no! Look at the enormous pawprints on the ground! This is a tiger's cave! The tiger will surely eat us when he returns!"

The father fox reassured her, "Don't worry. When the time comes, I will take care of the tiger."

Still, the mother fox insisted, "What exactly will we do when the tiger comes?"

"When he approaches, you must pinch the cubs until they cry," explained the father fox. "When I ask you what is wrong, you must reply that our children are hungry for a tiger."

The mother fox agreed to the plan, and soon the family was happily settled in their home. They lived there peacefully for a few days. But one evening, the mother fox spied the tiger returning. As planned, she began to pinch her cubs.

In a gruff voice, the father fox demanded, "Why are our children wailing?"

The mother fox replied brusquely, "They want to eat a tiger."

Hearing this exchange, the tiger stopped in his tracks. Thought he, "What creatures have entered my cave that even the babies feed on tigers? They must be fierce rakshash!"

From inside the cave, the father fox grumbled angrily, "Where am I supposed to get more tiger? Those greedy children have eaten up all that I brought them!"

His wife replied querulously, "I don't care where you go. You had better get another tiger, or your children won't stop crying."

"Wait a minute," the father fox shouted out, "I see a tiger just outside the cave. Hand me my jhaupaang, I'll go bhautaang him!"

Hearing those murderous-sounding words, the tiger feared for his life. "I may not know what those things are, but I'd better get out of here!" he thought to himself. He tucked his tail under him and fled rapidly into the deep forest.

A monkey sitting atop a tamarind tree saw the tiger bolting through the brush. There must be something wrong in the forest for a tiger to flee so! The monkey exclaimed, "Brother Tiger, Brother Tiger, what are you running from?"

The frightened tiger answered, "They were just about to eat me!"

The astounded monkey asked, "Who was going to eat you? In this great forest, there isn't a single creature big enough to harm you!"

"I wish you had been there," retorted the tiger, "then you would have believed it."

The monkey started laughing so hard, he almost fell off his branch. "Ha, ha ha! You are so stupid that no doubt someone has fooled you!"

"Who are you calling foolish?" exclaimed the angry tiger. "If you're so smart, why don't you come back with me to the cave?"

"Fine," agreed the monkey, "but only if you carry me on your back."

With the monkey on his back, the tiger bounded toward the cave again. In the meantime, the foxes had just settled down for a quiet evening with their cubs. They spotted the tiger returning, this time with a monkey.

Quickly, the mother fox began to pinch her young ones again. At their mother's sudden abuse, the cubs started howling at the top of their lungs.

In a harsh voice, the father fox bellowed, "Stop! Stop! Don't cry so much, you'll become ill."

The mother fox retorted fiercely, "I've told you a thousand times. Unless you feed them a tiger, these children won't stop screaming."

"I've just sent their uncle to fetch a tiger," shouted the father fox. "He'll be back in a minute. Now, tell them to shut up." He added loudly, "Oh, look. There comes your Uncle Monkey with a delicious tiger for you. Wife, hand me my jhaupaang, I'll go bhautaang him."

When the tiger heard these words, he was sure that the monkey had tricked him. With one huge leap, he shrugged the monkey off his shoulders and pelted away from the dangerous cave. He ran hard and fast for two days and nights, putting as much distance between him and the ferocious dwellers of the cave as possible.

The fox family knew that they would not have any more trouble from the tiger again.

TALES OF GREED AND PIETY

THE BRIDE'S LAMENT

Buzz! Buzz! Mosquitoes bite
Woe, that tiny pest
drove me to jungles deep
to find some peace and rest

The tiger in the woods did growl
Jumped I in the river
Crocodiles snapped at my heels
I fled home aquiver

At home, the maid did threaten so
my adventures she would tell
Off I ran into my room
Where Sis'-in-law did yell

From husband's sister I did flee
to cook the family meal
There, Ma-in-law was all ablaze
Before her I did kneel

Dearest mother, do not scold
Take your daughter's hand
Without your kindness, I am lost
with nowhere left to stand.

THE UNGRATEFUL TIGER

Once, a King in a faraway land had gone hunting in the forest. He caught the largest tiger anyone had ever seen, and kept it for display in a cage outside his palace. All day long, people would pass by the cage and stare at the ferocious beast. The tiger would humbly ask each passerby, "Won't you please open the cage door and release me?" And people would reply, "Do you take us for madmen? If we open the cage you will surely eat us." So, no one took it upon themselves to set the animal free.

One day, a kindly old Brahman teacher came to the palace to visit the King. As he passed the tiger cage, the animal called out piteously, "Oh, wise teacher, won't you hear my plea?" When the Brahman came near, the tiger meekly bowed his head and held out one big paw to touch his feet. He respectfully said, "Please, Master, just let me out of this cage once. Won't you please give me a taste of freedom?"

The Brahman was a studious man who spent all day amidst his books and papers. He knew little about life's practical matters. His gentle heart was moved at the tiger's plea for freedom, and so he opened the cage door.

But the tiger bounded out of his confines and leapt upon the poor Brahman. "Now, Master, I will eat you!" he announced.

The Brahman was thunderstruck at the tiger's audacity. "This is not done!" cried the unworldly teacher. "How can you repay my favor with cruelty?"

The tiger laughed scornfully, "That is the way of the world."

"That is just not true," argued the Brahman. "I am sure I can find you three witnesses to agree with me."

The tiger considered this proposal thoughtfully. "Alright," he finally said. "If three witnesses support you, then I will let you go. But if they agree with me, you will be my next meal."

The Brahman and the tiger walked to the nearest farm to find testifiers. Pointing to a lush green paddy field, the teacher said, "This field is my first witness."

The tiger approached the field and queried, "Tell me, if I help someone, will they harm me in return?"

The field responded angrily, "Of course they will. Look at me! I give the farmer such plentiful yield year after year. Yet he continuously abuses me by shredding me apart with his sharp plough. That is the way of the world."

The tiger looked at the teacher triumphantly. "You see, cruelty is the right repayment for kindness!"

The Brahman protested, "But I still have two more witnesses. We will see what they say."

At the far corner of the field, there grew a banyan tree. The Brahman pointed to it and declared, "That wise banyan will be my second witness."

They approached the ancient tree together and the tiger waved generously, "This time, why don't you ask the question?"

The Brahman asked, "Dear tree, you have lived a long time. You have seen and heard the ways of men. Tell me, is charity ever repaid with unkindness?"

The banyan replied, "As long as I have lived, that has been the way of the world. Look at me. People come and take shelter under my shady boughs. I protect them from torrential rains and the scorching sun. Yet, they tear off my leaves and chop down my branches."

The tiger licked his whiskers greedily. "Just like I told you, Master!" he growled.

Now, the Brahman became worried. He could not decide what to do next! Just then, he spotted a fox traveling by. Pointing to the animal, he said, "There is my third witness." He called out, "Master Fox, Master Fox, please stop! I want you to be my witness."

The fox halted, but would not agree to come any closer. "How is it that I am your witness?" he asked in puzzlement.

Like before, the Brahman asked, "Tell me, is generosity ever repaid with viciousness?"

The fox thought for some time, and then replied, "Only if I

108

hear more about the actual situation, who helped whom and who hurt whom in return, will I be able to make a decision."

The Brahman explained, "You see, this tiger was in a cage and I was walking on the path. . . ."

The fox interrupted smartly, "Then I must see this cage and this path!"

At this demand, all three returned to the palace walls. The fox examined the cage carefully, circling it twice. He muttered under his breath, "Okay, so the tiger was walking peacefully on the path and the Brahman was in the cage. . . ."

The tiger laughed out loud. "You silly fool! You have it all wrong. The tiger was in the cage and the Brahman was walking along the path."

"Oh, I understand now," said the fox. "The tiger was dressed as a Brahman and the path was inside the cage. . . ."

The tiger shouted impatiently, "No, stupid! The tiger inside the cage, the Brahman on the path. Do you understand?"

"Yes, yes, nothing could be simpler!" exclaimed the fox. "The Brahman was riding on the tiger down the path to buy a cage at the market."

The tiger roared in frustration, "I have never seen a more dimwitted fellow! Look, I will show you once and for all. The tiger was in the cage. . . ."

The tiger demonstrated by walking into the cage. As soon as he did so, the fox promptly slammed the door shut. The tiger was imprisoned again.

The fox said to the Brahman, "Master, I think I have finally grasped the situation. If you want this witness's opinion, it is this: Never help ungrateful creatures. That way, your kindness will never be returned with cruelty."

Gifts of kindness, special pearls
must not be strewn in dust
Such gifts must go to grateful souls
That is only just!

With these words, the fox ran into the forest; the Brahman went into the palace, and the tiger remained in his cage. That is the way of the world.

THE STEPMOTHER AND THE GODDESS

There once was a sea-trader whose wife had died, leaving him with a daughter and a son. After some time, the trader married again. His new wife bore him another son and daughter. The elder children were beloved by their father and all the other villagers. However, their stepmother could not stand the sight of them.

Soon, the trader was to leave on a long voyage. Knowing his wife's dislike of his elder children, he worried that his son and daughter would be neglected while he was gone. So, the trader went to the village milkman and baker to request that they look after his elder children. "Please feed them well, and I will repay you when I return," he begged. Happy with this secret arrangement, the trader went off to sea.

As soon as the trader left, the stepmother ordered her hated stepchildren to tend the livestock. The boy and girl were to take the cattle and goats to graze every day. Even though they worked long hours, the stepmother fed them only one meal of boiled rice. Despite her ill-treatment, the trader's elder children grew healthy and strong.

The stepmother wondered, "I feed my own children the best foods, yet they remain skin and bones. How do those two thrive on just hard work and meager food?" She sent her own children to spy on their elder brother and sister.

After a long day, all four children returned home. Immediately, the stepmother began scolding the elder two. Her own children exclaimed, "Ma, Ma, don't punish our elder brother and sister. Dada and Didi were so kind to us today. They fed us such delicious food as we have never tasted! And they eat that way every day!"

Hearing her children's explanations, the stepmother realized what her husband had arranged. She called the milkman and baker and ordered them to stop feeding her elder children. "My husband has written from sea. Two of his ships have sunk, and he is ill. He will not be able to pay you back for your expenses." Knowing how much the villagers loved her stepchildren, she then told all her neighbors, "Please don't feed my children. They become ill on your food."

From then on, no one in the village fed the elder children. Every day, the brother and sister grew more skinny and weak.

One day, while grazing the cattle, the brother and sister became so tired that they fell asleep. Upon awaking, they found that all of their animals had strayed. They searched all over the fields, but were unable to find any trace of their cows. Crying piteously, they went to a nearby house for help.

The wife of the house exclaimed, "Come in, dear children. There is a Natai-Chandi puja going on in our house. If you pray to the goddess, she will grant your wishes."

As they were told, the children prayed to the folk goddess, begging her to please return their cattle. Everyone laughed at their simple request, exclaiming, "Why don't you ask the goddess for your father's return? Ask her to bring your father home with fourteen shiploads of riches, diamond bangles, pearl necklaces, a wife and a husband for you to wed!"

The children prayed with all their hearts,

Natai-Chandi, village goddess,
powerful Mother divine
Hear our prayer, grant our wishes
We rely on goodness thine.

And the goddess was moved to pity.

Seeing the emaciated condition of the children, the wife of the house decided not to let them go back to their stepmother. After the puja, she invited them to stay with her family.

In the meantime, the sea-merchant returned home with fourteen shiploads of riches, diamond bangles, pearl necklaces, a wife and a husband for his eldest children to wed. The trader's wife began wailing at the sight of him, "Woe has befallen your household! Your elder children have been devoured by a tiger!"

The trader did not believe his wife's story. He immediately set out in search of his elder son and daughter. After a long day, he finally found the household that was sheltering his children. Joyously, he cradled them in his arms and set out for home.

The trader's wife was afraid that if her stepchildren returned, they would take the lion's share of the trader's newfound wealth. Quickly, she gathered up the money, jewels, gold and other riches the trader had brought home and started throwing the fortune into a covered well. But in her hurry, the evil stepmother slipped and fell headlong into the watery depths.

The trader came home and found his younger children alone. He realized his wife was gone. The next day, the sea-trader's elder daughter and son were married in a gala double ceremony. The elder son's kind and generous wife took over the duties of the household, caring for the younger children as if they were her own.

The family continued to pray to the goddess Natai-Chandi, who had brought them such fortune and joy. They lived happily for a very, very long time.

HOW OPIUM WAS MADE

A long time ago, on the banks of the River Ganges, there lived a sanyasi. The sanyasi spent long days in meditation and prayer. At night, he would retire to a hut he had built for himself out of palm leaves. Having renunciated all worldly attachments, he lived in simplicity, far from any other human being.

The sanyasi's only company was a mouse that lived in a dark corner of his hut. The holy man happily shared his meager food with the tiny animal. In time, the mouse learnt to trust him, sleeping by his side and playing around his feet. Since he had no other company, the sanyasi granted the animal the power to speak.

One evening, the mouse respectfully addressed the sanyasi. "Father, you have graciously allowed me the ability of speech. If I may, I would like to ask for one more favor."

"What would you like, my child?" asked the sanyasi.

The mouse replied, "Every day when you leave to bathe in the river, a cruel cat torments me. He has not devoured me up to now only because he fears you. I am afraid he may do so any day. Could you change me into a cat so that I can battle my enemy on equal grounds?"

The sanyasi was moved. He sprinkled some holy water upon the mouse, who was promptly changed into a long-whiskered feline.

After a few days, the sanyasi asked his beloved pet, "How are you doing, my kitty? Are you happy now?"

The cat complained, "Not really, Father. I have not yet found complete happiness."

"Why is that, my child?" inquired the sanyasi. "Are the other cats still troubling you?"

113

"Not at all, Sir," exclaimed the cat. "You have made me a mighty animal. There is no cat in this world that can defeat me. But, there is a new problem. When you go for your bath, a bunch of snarling dogs come to terrify me. If it is not too much of a bother, could you please turn me into a dog?"

The sanyasi granted the cat's wish.

Within a few days, the dog again approached his master. "Dear Father, due to your kindness I have gained much. I once was a mouse and you granted me speech. Then you made me a cat. Still I was not satisfied, so you made me a dog. Unfortunately, my troubles are not over. As a dog I find myself constantly hungry. The food left from your meals was enough for me as a mouse and even as a cat. For a large dog it is not enough." He continued sorrowfully, "It seems to me that the monkeys in the forest have a better life. They swing from tree to tree gathering fruits, and can eat all day. If you could give me a monkey's life, then I would be satisfied."

Immediately, the gentle sanyasi changed the dog into a monkey.

The monkey was at first joyous. He whooped from tree to tree feasting on the sweetest fruits. However, his luck soon ran out. That year, the monsoons did not come and the land fell into drought. The river and lakes dried up, and the monkey found himself unable to quench his thirst.

From the treetops, the monkey enviously watched the wild boars. They would dig into dried ponds and find water to drink. While the monkey's throat parched beneath a scorching sun, the boars rolled happily in cool, moist mud.

The monkey pleaded with the sanyasi again. "Oh, Father, you made me a monkey, but my fortune hasn't changed. I cannot find water to drink, yet I see the wild boars lolling about in wet mud all day. I do not mean to be demanding, but could you please change me into a boar?"

What endless patience! The sanyasi benevolently changed the monkey into a boar. Quite happily, the boar spent the next few days luxuriating at the bottom of the pond.

Soon, however, the forest was overrun by elaborately dressed elephants bearing a royal hunting party. When they came upon the pond, the hunters were elated to see so many wild boars in one place. Most of the animals met their doom at spear point. Somehow, the sanyasi's boar managed to evade destruction by hiding himself in the marshes.

After the hunters left, the boar contemplated. "What is the use of being a boar if my life becomes so full of danger? If I were a royal elephant, I could wear red silk and gold ornaments. I could carry the Raja himself on my back, and everyone would pay their respects when they saw me coming. Aha, if only I could be an elephant!"

That night, the boar went to the sanyasi and made his request. With disappointment in his eyes, the sanyasi relented, "So be it." The boar now turned into an elephant.

The elephant wandered through the forest, munching on a leafy branch here, a juicy banana plant there. Yet his greatest desire was to be the Raja's personal elephant. On the day the royal hunting party came to the forest, the elephant approached the group. Seeing him, the Raja exclaimed, "What a beautiful animal! Do not harm it. If I could tame that elephant, I would make it my own."

The royal hunters had no difficulty in capturing the elephant and taking him to the palace. Whoever saw him would remark, "What a majestic creature!", and the elephant beamed with pride.

One day, the Raja and Rani were going to the Ganges for a purifying bath. The Raja expressed his desire to travel upon the new elephant, and commanded his mahout to adorn the animal in royal finery. The elephant was ecstatic. However, his joy was diminished by the presence of the Rani. He thought, "She may be a Queen and all, but she is little more than a woman! Why should I have to carry her upon my back? I am the king of animals, and I should only have to carry a King."

With this thought, the elephant reared up on his hind legs, and off fell the Raja and Rani. The Raja picked himself up quickly and cradled his wife in his arms. He dusted her face and hands with his own silk robe, asking, "My dearest, are you hurt? I couldn't bear it if anything happened to you."

115

The elephant watched this exchange with amazement, and thought, "How lucky the Queen is! The Raja loves her so much, he holds her life more precious than his own! There must be no joy greater than being a Queen."

The elephant went back to the sanyasi sobbing piteously. The sanyasi asked worriedly, "What's the matter now? Aren't you happy as the royal elephant?"

The elephant bowed low, "Father, you have always granted my wishes. Your kindness knows no bounds. However, I have this one last request, then I vow never to ask you for anything again." The elephant continued, "Although I am large in size as an elephant, my happiness has not grown proportionately. I believe there is no one as happy as a Queen in this world. Please, Father, make me a Rani."

Laughingly, the sanyasi replied, "You silly child, how can I make you a Rani? A Queen must have a kingdom, and more importantly, a husband who is a King. I cannot give you all that. The most I can do for you is to make you a woman of incomparable beauty. Maybe then a King will be so overcome by you that he will take you as his wife, and your wish will come true.

The elephant agreed, "Alright then, make me a woman of perfection."

With a sprinkle of holy water, the sanyasi instantly turned the elephant into a radiant beauty. He named his newly born daughter Precious-Poppy.

From then on, Precious-Poppy lived with the sanyasi in his forest hut. She planted a lush garden of colorful flowers which she tended day and night.

One morning, when the sanyasi was away and Poppy was sitting in her garden, a man attired in gorgeous robes came up to her. "Why are you here, Sir?" asked Poppy, rising from her seat.

The stranger replied, "I was hunting in the forest when I spotted the most astonishing deer. I followed it and became separated from my party. Now, I have not only lost the deer but am dying of thirst. Dear lady, could you give me a cool drink of water?"

116

HOW OPIUM WAS MADE

Precious-Poppy had already recognized the Raja. She invited him politely to come inside. "Your Majesty, we are but poor people; anything we have is yours."

The Raja thought to himself, "She is so beautiful and gracious, she must be the daughter of a King!" Aloud, he queried, "Who is your father, beautiful lady?"

Cleverly, Poppy answered, "Although I live with the sanyasi, he is but my adopted father. I have heard from him that my real father was a King. Vanquished by enemies, my father and mother took refuge in the forest. Here I was born. Unable to take care of me, they left me beneath a banyan tree. The branches of the tree shaded me and the roots were my cradle. There was a honeycomb above my head which nursed me with drops of honey. My sanyasi father found me thus."

The Raja immediately begged, "Princess of the forest, I will be honored if you would marry me."

The sanyasi returned to his hut to find the Raja and his beaming daughter. Unable to deny his beloved child anything, he readily agreed to the marriage. Joyously, the Raja returned to his palace with his new bride.

As you might have guessed by now, this was the same Raja whose Rani had fallen off the elephant's back. With the arrival of Precious-Poppy, the elder Rani was pushed to one side. While Poppy became the favored wife of the Raja, his once beloved Rani was abandoned in a neglected corner of the palace.

But Precious-Poppy's luck did not hold for long. Strolling in the palace courtyard one day, she came upon a well. Enamored with her own beautiful reflection, vain Poppy leaned too far and fell in. No one was able to save her.

Beside himself with sorrow, the Raja went to the sanyasi to seek solace. The holy man consoled him, "Dear Raja, do not grieve for your wife. Poppy has lived out her own destiny." Then he told the Raja all about Poppy's transformations. "Your wife was once a small mouse in my cottage. I gave him the power to speak. At his request, I changed him into a cat, a dog, a monkey, a wild boar and then, into an elephant. Lastly, I turned him into the fair maiden who became your wife." Smiling at the Regent's amazement, the sanyasi added, "Do not mourn

Precious-Poppy's death. Treat your first wife with kindness and respect, as you have been unjust to her."

Still, the King's sadness was immeasurable. The sanyasi finally said, "I will give you something by which to remember my daughter. From the well where Poppy died will burst forth a plant with beautiful white flowers. The seeds of these flowers will give birth to something called opium. Like a father's love, it will have the power to heal, but people will also abuse it. Anyone who takes opium will thus suffer through all Poppy's incarnations. He will be restless as a mouse, will love milk like a cat, will be querulous as a dog, dirty as a monkey, ferocious as a wild boar, unresponsive as an elephant, and arrogant as a queen."

And so opium came to life.

THE GODDESS OF CHILDREN

In a forest of ashok trees, there lived a sanyasi. One morning, when the sanyasi was walking through the woods, he came upon a little girl as pretty as a lotus bud. The child was lying under a blossoming ashok tree, wailing in hunger. The gentle sanyasi gathered the little girl in his arms and took her back to his hut. He named her Ashoka, after the benevolent tree which had sheltered her. From then on, the holy man brought her up as his own daughter.

But who were Ashoka's real parents? How could the lone sanyasi take care of this suckling infant? In a meditative trance, the sanyasi learned that the little girl was the child of a deer. When he was away from the hut, the deer would come to nurse her daughter. In this way, the girl grew into a beautiful young woman. It was time for her to get married. The sanyasi began searching for a husband for Ashoka. However, as soon as the suitors heard that she was borne by a deer, they declined her hand. Frustrated by repeated rejections, the sanyasi finally vowed, "Whoever I see first tomorrow morning will be Ashoka's husband."

The next day, the sanyasi awoke to find a handsome Prince standing at the door of his hut. The young Prince explained, "I had come to hunt in the forest yesterday, but became separated from my party. May I bother you for a drink of water?"

The sanyasi took him into the hut and gave him fruits and water. Pleased with the young man's respectful behavior, he said, "I have a young daughter who is very beautiful. I would like you to marry her."

When the Prince saw Ashoka, he became enchanted by her loveliness. He agreed readily to be her husband. Under the boughs

119

of an ashok tree, the sanyasi married the happy couple. Before Ashoka left for the Prince's kingdom, her father presented her with a handful of dried ashok flowers and seeds. "My child, eat these flowers in the month of Chaitra, on the day the Goddess of Children is worshiped. On that day of Ashok Shashti puja, never eat any rice," he added, "and sprinkle these ashok seeds on your way from my forest hut to the royal palace. If ever you are in any danger, follow the tree-lined path back to me."

Ashoka complied with her father's instructions, trailing seeds from the hut all the way to the palace. There she settled down happily with her in-laws, the Raja and Rani. But true to her word, in the month of Chaitra, on the day of Ashok Shashti puja, she ate the ashok flowers but took no rice. In this way, Ashoka bore the Prince seven sons and a daughter.

Many years passed. Ashoka's children grew strong and healthy, and were eventually all married. The old Raja and Rani passed away, leaving the kingdom to Ashoka's husband. As the new Rani, Ashoka's devotion to the Goddess of Children made her people flourish.

*   *   *

One day, in the month of Chaitra, on the day of Ashok Shasti puja, Ashoka told her sons' wives, "Today I worship the Goddess of Children. I will eat no rice." So her daughters-in-law prepared for her a meal of ashok flowers and soaked lentils.

The next day, Ashoka awoke to a still kingdom. Everyone throughout the palace and countryside had died in the night. Unable to understand why fate had dealt her such a cruel blow, Ashoka was beside herself with grief. Then she remembered the words of her father, the sanyasi. She followed the path to his hut, which was now lined by tall ashok trees.

Ashoka threw himself, sobbing, at the sanyasi's feet. "Father, Father, what has happened? Why am I cursed so?" she cried.

The sanyasi went into a meditative trance to seek the truth. When he opened his eyes, he informed Ashoka, "In the soaked lentils that your daughters-in-law prepared, there was one kernel of rice. You were not careful, and ate this taboo food. That is why your kingdom is in ruins."

Ashoka pleaded, "I was wrong, Father, to be so negligent. It will never happen again. Please restore my people to me."

"Alright," the sanyasi consented. He gave his daughter a pot of holy water and said, "Go sprinkle this water around your kingdom, and all will be well. From now on, in the month of Chaitra, during the waxing phase of the moon, you must fast every day. Every evening, you must worship the Goddess of Children with lentils and ashok buds. Only then can you break your fast. And remember, never let your lips touch rice on the Ashok Shashti day."

Ashoka sprinkled the holy water around the kingdom, rejoicing as her beloved people were returned to life. The royal family too was revived. They were amazed to hear Ashoka's story. The Raja ordered that all the women of his land must follow their Rani in worshiping the Goddess of Children on the day of Ashok Shashti.

TWO SISTERS

There was once a weaver who had two wives. Each wife had one daughter. The weaver preferred his eldest wife and her daughter, Sukhu. Although both were mean and idle, he showered them with love and affection. Neither Sukhu nor her mother would lift a finger to help around the house, but lazed from morning until night stuffing themselves with food. On the other hand, the weaver's younger wife and her daughter Dukhu would spin cotton, clean the weaver's home, cook, and serve Sukhu and her mother. Only then were they allowed their daily allowance of food.

Then, the weaver died. Right away, the elder wife claimed all his money, turning out his second wife and daughter from their home.

One day Sukhu's mother would bring home the largest fish from the market; the next day she would bring the freshest vegetables. She would cook up savory meals for herself and her daughter, eating them with relish. Of course, she made sure her banished co-wife and step-daughter knew of these feasts.

Next door, in a poorly-built, ramshackle hut, Dukhu and her mother would spin cotton until their fingers bled. But no matter how hard they worked, they only managed to weave a tiny towel here, a handkerchief there. By selling those pieces, they were just able to afford one measly meal per day.

One morning, Dukhu and her mother awoke to find their spindle cotton soaked from the rainwater that had leaked through the roof. Putting out the cotton to dry in the sun, Dukhu's mother went to bathe in the river. Dukhu was left to watch over the precious material. Suddenly, a gust of wind swept the wispy cotton high into the air. Poor Dukhu ran after the errant

122

threads, but was not able to catch even the smallest handful. Finally, she collapsed upon the ground, sobbing piteously. The wind comforted the little girl, "Dukhu, don't cry. Come with me, and I will give you all the cotton you want." Still wiping her eyes, Dukhu followed the breeze.

On the way, a cow called out, "Dukhu, where are you going? Will you clean my shed for me?" Kind Dukhu was not able to deny the animal's request. She swept the shed clean, piled fresh hay for the cow to eat, and filled its trough with cool water. Then, she started again on her mission.

A few steps down the road, a banana plant asked, "Dukhu, where are you going? My trunk is covered with twisted vines. You can take them down for me?" Dukhu happily did as the plant bid.

A little while later, a thorn tree called out, "Dukhu, where are you going? My base is crowded with fallen leaves. Will you sweep them clean for me?" Braving the thorny branches, Dukhu put the tree to rights before heading off after the wind.

Then a horse neighed to her, "Dukhu, Dukhu, where are you going? Will you gather a little sweet grass for me to eat?" Without complaining, Dukhu halted again, not resuming her journey until she had gathered a mountain of downy grass for the horse.

The gusty breeze led Dukhu on a windy journey, down paths that seemed to lead forever. Finally, she came upon a shining white house circled by airy verandas. Although the house looked uninhabited, the enormous rooms sparkled spick-and-span, and the lush gardens seemed well taken care of. In the central court-yard of the house, Dukhu came upon an old woman who was spinning endlessly. In the blink of an eye, she would weave a hundred thousand shimmering saris. The breeze whispered, "Dukhu, this is old Mother of the Moon. Ask her for your cotton and you will get it."

Touching the old woman's feet respectfully, Dukhu said, "Ayi-Ma, the wind has stolen all my cotton. My mother will scold me for losing it. Please, Ayi-Ma, can you get it back for me?"

The old lady, Mother of the Moon, had hair like the froth of fresh milk. It glowed like the light of a full moon. Pushing it away from her eyes, she looked up from her spinning. Before her was a little girl with words as sweet as melting honey. The old woman said, "Come, my golden child. In the other room is a soft towel, a sari, and some hair oil. Take these and dip twice into that yonder pond. Have something to eat, and then we will find your cotton."

In the room, Dukhu found piles of soft towels and the richest of silken saris. She pushed these aside, and took for herself a simple garment of cotton and an old and tattered towel. Putting the smallest drop of oil upon her hair, she went to bathe in the pond. The first time she dipped into the water, Dukhu became more beautiful than even a devi. But little Dukhu did not realize her beauty. At the second dip, Dukhu's body became covered with golden jewelry. From head to foot, she sparkled. Dukhu then went off to eat, as the old woman had bid. The dining room was filled with such delicacies as she had never seen before, but Dukhu sat in a corner, eating nothing but a little rice with salt. Then she returned to the old Mother of the Moon.

The old woman said, "Come, my little golden baby. Go to that room at the far end of the house and you will find a trunk filled with cotton."

Dukhu went as she was told, and found not one, but hundreds of different trunks of all shapes and sizes. From the darkest corner of the room, she picked out a tiny trunk, almost like a toy box, and returned to the side of the old lady.

The old Mother of the Moon said, "My little treasure, go home to your mother. This trunk holds your cotton."

Bidding farewell respectfully to the old woman, Dukhu started back home. Her beauty and jewels lit the way for her through the darkness.

The horse whom she had helped called out, "Dukhu, Dukhu, how can I repay your kindness? Here is a little token of my gratitude." He presented Dukhu with a graceful winged horse.

The thorn tree then said, "Dukhu, what else can I give you? Here, have this pitcher full of gold coins."

The banana plant offered, "Here, take these bunches of golden bananas."

The cow said, "Dukhu, take this little cow home. She will always give you the sweetest of milk."

124

Carrying her trunk and newfound treasures, Dukhu arrived home.

In the meantime, her mother had been frantically searching for her. Seeing her precious child, Dukhu's mother ran to embrace her, crying, "Oh, where have you been, my child? You are the light in this darkness." Seeing Dukhu laden with such invaluable gifts, she cried out in alarm, "Oh, daughter of a poor woman, from where you have brought all these priceless riches?"

After Dukhu had told her mother about her adventures, the younger wife of the weaver ran to her old home. "Sister, sister," she called, "see what Dukhu has brought back from the old Mother of the Moon. Let Sukhu share in these gifts."

Twisting her face and scowling viciously, Sukhu's mother retorted, "Sharing in a pauper's treasure? My daughter is of better measure!" She slammed her door on Dukhu and her mother.

That night, when Dukhu and her mother returned to their shack, they decided to open the old woman's tiny trunk. They were thunderstruck when a handsome Prince stepped out of the magic trunk and asked for Dukhu's hand in marriage. Immediately, the shack became a splendid palace where Dukhu, her princely husband and her mother lived in joy. From then on, the Prince rode upon the winged horse, the mother tended the gentle cow, and sweet Dukhu kept her royal home with great delight.

*   *   *

The next day, Sukhu's mother bolted and locked her front door, spread out a bale of cotton in her backyard, and went to bathe in the pond. Before she left, she whispered some secret instructions to her daughter. "Phish . . . phish . . . phish." In a little while, the breeze came and blew away all the cotton. Sukhu dashed after the wind.

On her way, the cow called out, "Sukhu, where are you going? Will you stop a moment for me?" But Sukhu ran on, ignoring the request. The banana plant, the thorn tree, the horse all called after Sukhu, but she had no time for them either.

125

She yelled out to them over her shoulder, "I'm going to the see the old lady, the Mother of the Moon! Why should I have to stop for you?"

Chasing the wind, Sukhu finally arrived at the old woman's home. Without pausing to look at the beautiful surroundings, she bustled into the central courtyard and marched straight up to the Mother of the Moon. "Hey, old lady!" she called out rudely, "stop your useless spinning and give me all my things! You gave so much to that little twit, Dukhu, you better give me even more!" With these harsh words, Sukhu pulled the distaff out of the old woman's hands and knocked over her spinning wheel.

The old Mother of the Moon cried out in alarm. "Stop, stop! Such a little girl, and such big words!" She gazed thoughtfully at Sukhu, before adding, "Alright, you'll get your things, but first why don't you take a bath and have a little food?"

Sukhu ransacked the room for the most gorgeous silk sari and the softest of towels. She grabbed the most fragrant hair oil and a bowlful of sandalwood paste before heading off to bathe. The first dip was beauty. The second brought her jewels. Sukhu jumped in joy and thought, "The more I dip into this magic pond, the more splendid I will become!"

"Ayi-ayi-ayi!" After the third dip, Sukhu yelled in dismay. Her body was covered with warts and blisters, bumps and rashes. Her nails grew like talons, her hair stuck out like brittle hay. Sukhu gazed into the water and met her reflection—an ugly crone! Crying, "Oh Ma'go! Oh Baba-re!" Sukhu ran back to the old Mother of the Moon.

Seeing her, the old woman exclaimed sorrowfully, "Oh, my unfortunate dear! Did you dip three times? Oh well, don't cry now. Why don't you at least get something to eat?"

Raining curses on the old woman's head, Sukhu stomped off to the dining room. There, she gobbled up the best sweetmeats, and scattered the remains of her half-eaten meal all over the beautiful room. Then she washed her face and hands and returned to the courtyard, "I want to go back to my mother now, old woman. Give me the trunk you promised!"

Wordlessly, the old Mother of the Moon pointed Sukhu in

the direction of the trunk room. Unlike her sister, Sukhu chose the largest trunk she could possibly carry. Balancing it precariously on her head, she headed home, still cursing the old woman's name. At the sight of Sukhu, foxes ran away and villagers swooned. The horse gave her a swift kick, and Sukhu cried out, "Ayi! Ayi!" A branch from the thorn tree broke off and landed upon her, the banana plant dropped a heavy bunch of fruit upon her back, and the cow chased Sukhu all the way home.

In the meantime, Sukhu's mother had decorated their house in honor of her daughter's triumphant return. Placing two golden thrones on the veranda, she awaited expectantly. Seeing her daughter, Sukhu's mother cried out, "Oh, Ma! What will become of us? Where will we go?" and promptly fainted.

After waking, Sukhu's mother mourned, "Oh, well. What else is there to do? Perhaps things will improve when your husband emerges from the magic trunk." That night, the mother and daughter opened the trunk to find Sukhu's groom.

And oh, Ma! Who do you suppose it was? The most enormous python you have ever seen slithered out of the trunk and swallowed Sukhu and Sukhu's mother whole. No one ever saw them again.

A TALE OF TWO THIEVES

Many, many years ago, in a certain faraway village, there lived two thieves. Whenever the villagers lost anything they would blame the two thieves for stealing it, whether they were guilty or not. Finally, the thieves grew tired of being blamed for crimes they had not committed. So, they decided to give up thievery. They packed up some belongings, promising to send soon for their families, and went in search of honest employment.

They were soon employed in a farmer's household. The elder thief was hired to water the champak tree, and the younger was supposed to tend the farmer's cow.

The farmer told the elder thief, "You must water the champak tree until a pool of water collects around its base. Make sure you do not stop until then." The thief woke before dawn, and poured bucket after bucket of water around the tree. The ground instantly soaked up all the liquid he poured. No matter how much he watered, the base of the tree remained dry. After a whole day of such efforts, the exhausted thief fell asleep.

The younger thief's luck was no better. The cow he was supposed to tend was notoriously uncontrollable. As soon as the thief set it to graze in the pasture, the cow promptly turned tail and ran. All day, the cow ran about, destroying a paddy field here, munching on sugar cane there. Unable to catch the animal, the local farmers cursed the cowherd for his carelessness. The poor thief's day was spent chasing the cow from one field into another, through ponds and over pastures. Not only that, but he had to fend off the abuse of angry farmers. At last, by evening, the thief caught the mischievous cow and returned home.

Seeing him, the elder thief asked, "What took you so long, Brother?"

"What can I tell you, Dada?" the younger thief responded. "I took the cow to the pasture, where she contentedly grazed near a cool river. So obedient was she that I laid down under a shady tree by the banks and fell asleep. Awaking only after sundown, I caught the gentle cow and brought her home. How was your day?"

"Great!" the elder thief replied. "I only had to pour one bucket of water under the champak tree for a pool to form around the base. My work done, I wandered here and there, whistling a happy tune. I too fell asleep, and was just waking up when you arrived."

After hearing each other's stories, the thieves became convinced that the other's task was the easier one. Silently, both plotted to exchange chores for the next day. The elder thief said slyly, "Brother, I would really like to tend the cow tomorrow. Do you mind if we exchange jobs?"

The younger thief replied, "Not at all, Dada! It would be fun to see what your job is like. But let me give you a piece of advice: make sure you take a cot with you tomorrow. Lying on the hard ground all day will make your body ache."

The next day, the elder thief slung a cot over his shoulder and headed off to the pasture with the farmer's cow. In the meantime, the younger thief began watering the champak tree. Believing that the tree only needed a couple of buckets of water, he was amazed to find the base dry even after a hundred buckets. After toiling all day in this manner, he finally gave up, exhausted.

The elder thief's day was no better. As soon as he set the cow free by the river, it ran swiftly in the other direction. He spent his whole day running after the errant animal, and fending off angered farmers. Not only that, but his ordeal was made more difficult by the heavy cot. At the sight of a grown man dashing here and there after a cow while dragging a heavy cot around, all the other cowherds laughed uproariously. It was after sundown by the time the elder thief caught the animal and headed home.

Upon seeing each other, the two thieves began to laugh. The younger thief inquired, "So, Dada, how was your day?"

The elder thief answered, "Exactly like yours, my brother."

The younger thief exclaimed, "Hai Ram! And this is called an honest day's work? Don't you think our old profession was much better than this torment?"

The elder thief agreed, "Absolutely! I have never seen a more disobedient animal than this farmer's cow."

"I am sure we could find worse cows than this one," the younger thief said. "But have you ever heard of such a thirsty tree? Where does all that water go? There must be an ocean flowing beneath the farmer's champak."

"You're probably right," nodded the elder thief. "We should dig the tree up to see what's there under its roots."

The younger suggested, "Let's do it right now while everyone in the farmer's household is fast asleep."

With shovels and pickaxes in hand, the two thieves began to dig up the champak tree. After a while, the younger thief's tool hit a hard object. What excitement! Both thieves dug furiously and soon uncovered a brass pot. Upon putting his hand inside the pot, the younger thief discovered it was filled with gold coins. However, the elder thief could not see the treasure in the dark.

Quickly the younger thief removed his hand and remarked, "Darn it! There is nothing but stones in this pot!"

The elder thief did not for a moment believe his friend's words. However, he did not voice his suspicions.

Both agreed, "If there is nothing of gain here, why should we continue to dig?" They collected their tools and went home to sleep.

In a couple of hours the younger thief was sound asleep. The elder one tiptoed past him and returned to the champak tree. He dug up the brass pot and found it to be full of gold. Digging a bit further, he uncovered a similar pot filled with gold coins. He thought to himself, "I must hide these pots in a safe place." He took both pots and buried them in the soft soil by the farmer's pond. He then returned home quietly to find his friend still sleeping.

The younger thief woke in the wee hours of the morning and went to dig up his treasure. When he could not find the pot of gold, he realized it must be the handiwork of his friend. "Now, where has he hidden it?" wondered the younger thief. He returned to his sleeping friend in search of clues and found some soft mud on the elder thief's heels.

"Aha!" thought the younger thief. "He has hidden the gold by the pond. But where, and on which bank?"

Cleverly, the younger thief started walking around the pond. As he passed by each bank, he noticed that startled frogs jumped into the pond. However, on the west side, the frogs were already in the water. "Someone must have already disturbed them," concluded the younger thief. "This is where the gold is buried."

It did not take the younger thief long to find the treasure; not one but two pots of gold. He took the pots to the cowshed where he tied them on the back of the farmer's cow. Leading the animal by its noose, he headed for his village.

With the first light of the morning, the elder thief was awake. When he saw his friend's empty bed, he knew there was trouble. He ran to the pond only to discover that the pots of gold were missing. Then he went to the cowshed and found that the cow was missing as well. He realized that the younger thief must have loaded the gold on the animal's back and left for home. Immediately, he set out on the path to catch his friend.

On his way, the elder thief passed a shop selling beautiful nagra shoes. He quickly bought a pair before heading off down backroads and alleyways toward home. In a little while, he spied the younger thief ahead of him. Confident of a clean getaway, the younger thief was taking his own sweet time, meandering slowly down the village path. Avoiding the main road, the elder thief cut across a field and stopped around a bend, ahead of the younger thief. He placed one of the nagra shoes in the middle of the road and ran on. After another stretch, he placed the other shoe beneath a tree. Then, climbing up on a branch, he hid himself and waited.

In the meantime, the younger thief had come upon the first nagra. "What a gorgeous shoe!" he exclaimed. "Now that I am a rich man, it is only fitting that I have such footwear. But, what will I do with only one?" With these words, he continued on.

After a little while, the younger thief found the second nagra. "Oh, Ma!" he said. "What a fool I am! I should have picked up the first shoe when I saw it. Well, it's not too far. I'll go back and collect it." He tied the cow to the tree and started back.

As soon as the younger thief was out of sight, the elder one climbed down from the tree. He untied the cow and headed home down backroads.

When the younger thief returned with his new pair of shoes, the cow was gone. Realizing who had taken the animal, he dashed back to the village. He went directly to the elder thief's house and waited for him to arrive.

When the elder thief came home with the gold-bearing cow, his friend was there to greet him. "I see you've made it safely home, Dada," said the younger thief. "Why don't we go inside and divide up all our newfound money?"

The elder thief agreed.

In the courtyard of the elder thief's home, the two friends unloaded the brass pots from the cow's back. Locking themselves into a room, they began to divvy up the gold coins. One coin to the elder and one to the younger; so went the process until both pots were empty. In the end, there was only one coin left.

Who was to get the last coin? In the spirit of compromise, the thieves decided they would cash the coin for silver and split the money equally. Since it was far too late to do so, an argument ensued about where the gold piece should be kept for the night. After much debate, it was decided that the coin would remain with the elder thief and be exchanged for silver in the morning.

As soon as the younger thief left, the elder called to his wife and daughters. He explained, "Tomorrow morning my friend will come for his share of the gold piece. I have no intention of giving it to him." He laid out a plan to his family. "Tomorrow, I will lie in the courtyard, pretending to be dead. To make it convincing, you must put a tulsi plant by my head and wail terribly when he comes. If he finds me dead, he won't bother anymore for his share of the money!" The women agreed.

Early the next morning, the younger thief rushed to collect

132

his share. As he approached the elder thief's house, he heard women crying. He hurried into the courtyard and discovered a shrouded body laid out beneath a tulsi plant.

Then the elder thief's wife was clutching at him, her eyes red from weeping. She demanded, "Where did you two go that my poor husband caught such an illness? He returned to me only to die last night!"

But the younger thief knew his friend too well! He quickly realized what was going on. Putting on a face of mourning, he said, "I am so sorry! My brother, my friend, has left this earth. Don't worry, I will take care of his funeral."

With these words, he began to drag the elder thief's prone body toward the cremation grounds. Upside down, the elder thief bumped over every stone and brick in the road. Yet he bit his lips to keep from crying out in pain. He could not reveal that he was alive for fear of sharing the last coin.

Once they reached the cremation grounds, the younger thief tied his friend by the heels to a tree branch. Climbing high into the tree, he waited for the elder thief to give up his pretense. How long could anyone remain hanging upside down, playing dead? But the elder thief was determined not to lose his money. Night soon fell upon the two friends.

On their way to rob a house, a group of dacoits came upon the hanging body. The head dacoit cried out, "What a good omen! It is very lucky to see a dead body on our way to work. I vow, if we are successful tonight, we will give this man a proper funeral."

Still, the elder thief was silent.

In the early hours of the morning, the dacoits returned to the tree, rich with stolen booty. True to his word, the head dacoit made a funeral pyre and laid the body upon it. As soon as he lit the kindling, the elder thief leaped up with a mighty yell. At the same time, the younger thief jumped down from the tree with a triumphant whoop. Thinking they were besieged by ghosts, the frightened dacoits ran for their lives.

The two thieves collected the dacoits' spoils and went home, arm in arm. They split the money in two equal halves and began leading happy lives.

133

TALES OF THE SUPERNATURAL

THE GHOST IN THE TREE

There is an old man on a coconut tree
He catches bad children, will not set them free
Like long white radishes, two teeth hang
His back's like a drum that no one dares bang
Floppy ears waggle in the north breeze
His eyes blaze like coals that make your blood freeze
A knotty old rope twists round his waist
He wanders through homes for children to taste
The boys who wail, he throws in a pail
He'll box their ears with ghostly sneers

Be careful, you children from far and from near
Make sure, when you cry, the old man doesn't hear!

THE DEMON SLAYERS

There was a Raja with two Ranis. One of the Ranis was a rakshashi, but no one knew that. Each Rani had a son. The good, human Rani's son was Kusum and the rakshashi Rani's son was Ajit. Ajit and Kusum, the two brothers, were the best of friends.

The rakshashi Rani's heart was black, her tongue bloody red with greed. She could not tolerate the friendship of Ajit and Kusum. Impatiently, she counted the days until she could make a savory curry with Kusum's flesh and bones. But the son of her womb would never leave the side of her co-wife's offspring. So all the rakshashi could do was to grind her teeth in perpetual anger.

As the rakshashi waited for an opportunity to get her hands on Kusum, she drained blood from the human Rani with her eyes. Within days, the elder Rani grew pale and took to her bed. Her hunger for Kusum's tender flesh growing every day, the rakshashi licked her lips in the shadow of her veil. Soon, the gentle and pious Rani died, and the entire kingdom was drowned in grief.

Now, the rakshashi shoved Ajit aside and cursed Kusum to die. She damned her stepson thirty-six times over, while banishing her own son to the darkest corner of the palace. The iron heart of Ajit was strong enough to withstand such abuse, but the golden heart of Kusum shattered from the pain. Within days, Kusum began to wither. Ajit wiped the tears from his older brother's eyes. "Dada," he promised, "we'll never go near Ma again."

"What?" the Rani exclaimed. "The son of my own womb has become my enemy?" Her heart burst into angry flames. That night, all the royal elephants died, the Raja's horses collapsed

137

and his precious cattle perished. There was a stench of death throughout the stables. The kingdom was astounded at the mysterious events.

The very next night, a ferocious din awoke the Raja in his bedchamber: *Kayi-maai! Kayi-maai!* The Raja hurried to check on his sons. Over the golden bed where the young Princes slept loomed a fearsome rakshash who had picked Kusum up by the throat like a wooden doll. Before the Raja even had a chance to move, the Rani leapt out of a dark corner of the room. Ripping out a handful of her own hair, she flung it at the Raja. In an instant, he became paralyzed. As the rakshash started to eat Kusum, he watched helplessly. And all the time, the Rani laughed in bubbly glee.

Ajit awoke. The night was dark, something was wrong. Why wasn't his brother next to him? He got up to find the air trembling ominously, the bangles on his mother's arm rattling viciously. A rakshash was eating his brother! With eyes blazing, Ajit struck the rakshash with his bare hand. Screaming *"Ayi-ayi!"* in pain, the demon vomited up a golden ball and ran for his life.

The rakshashi Rani realized that the order of the world had turned upside down. Her own son had become her adversary. Her mind burning in rage, she quickly chewed up and swallowed Ajit. But she could not digest her willful son, and vomited up an iron ball. With trembling knees and queasy stomach, the rakshashi gathered the gold and iron balls and climbed up to the highest terrace of the palace.

The royal terraces were filled with the Rani's rakshash relatives. On the left, they clamored, *"Huum-huum khaam!* Let's plunder and roam!" On the right, they cried, *"Guum-guum gaam!* Let's head for home!" The Rani replied, *"Gob-gob gum! Khom-khom khaak!* I'll stay here, you go back!" The palace shook, the Raja trembled, the forest uprooted itself and the rivers boiled as all the rakshash flew back to Demon-Land.

Within the palace, the Rani found no comfort. Her heart and feet burned in agony. She had to get rid of the gold and iron balls. Climbing upon a storm cloud, she rode all the way to the river and buried the gold and iron balls beside the bamboo forest. Feeling better, she headed home. Busy with her work, she did not notice the ominous signs of a crow shrieking and a fox howling.

Soon after, a farmer who had gone to the riverside to cut bamboo sticks found two strange-looking balls. "They must be snake eggs," he thought, and went to throw them away. But the eggs burst open and two Princes emerged: one blue, one red. With crowns on their heads and swords in their hands, the twin Princes walked swiftly toward the royal city. The astounded farmer was left staring at the empty shells upon the ground. With the iron shell, he cast himself a new sickle and plowshare. With the golden shell, he made his wife and daughter-in-law new armlets and belts.

In the meantime, the Princes had reached an enormous city that was being terrorized by groups of marauding khokkosh. The poor Raja of the realm would appoint a new minister every day, and every day, the khokkosh would devour not only the minister but one entire family of subjects. The harassed Raja had declared that if any twin Princes could rid his land of the khokkosh, he would not only give them his kingdom, but the hands of his beautiful twin daughters in marriage. Although many scores of Princes had attempted the feat, all had been torn apart by sharp khokkosh teeth.

The red and blue Princes, Lalkamal and Neelkamal, told the beleaguered Raja, "We will rid your land of khokkosh." Without daring to hope, the Raja gave his consent. As the night fell, Lalkamal and Neelkamal locked themselves within the palace store-room and waited with unsheathed swords. But by midnight, no one had come, and the brothers grew sleepy. Neel told his elder brother, "Dada, you take the first watch. Wake me in two hours and then I will take over. But," he added, "should the khokkosh come and ask who you are, remember to say my name first."

Soon after, there was a knock at the door. Prince Lal sat alert. As you know, khokkosh cannot see very clearly in the light, so they called, "Put out the light!" Knowing their tricks, Lal refused, "No, never, I won't!" Fuming, the head khokkosh growled, "Is that so? Who stays awake in this darkest hour?"

139

And all the other khokkosh chorused, "Who's awake? Who's awake?"

Lal replied,

Before Neel, awake is Lal
Alert with every breath
The light is strong, the sword is sharp
Who is courting death?

Hearing Neelkamal's name uttered, the khokkosh retreated three paces. As you know, Neelkamal was born in the womb of a rakshashi queen, and had rakshash blood coursing through his veins. Of course, the khokkosh knew this as well. They held an impromptu meeting and finally decided that they would test to see whether the voice they heard was really Neel's.

The head khokkosh called out, "Alright, let's see your nails!" Cleverly, Lal edged out the point of Neel's crown through a crack in the door. Since the khokkosh are not a very bright species, they were quite fooled by the sharp tip of the crown. *"Baap-re!"* they cried, taking turns examining the sharp point. "How strong must the owner of this fingernail be!"

But the head khokkosh was not convinced. He called out, "Alright, let's see your spit!" This time, Lal took the boiling oil from the lamp and splattered the khokkosh with it. *"Ayi! Kayi!"* they cried, as their fur singed and burned.

But the head khokkosh, who was an inquisitive fellow, persisted. "Stick out your tongue for us!" he cried. Lal swiftly extended the sharp edge of Neel's sword through the door crack. The head khokkosh grabbed the sword with both hands and declared, "This time, we'll pull out his tongue!" He told the other khokkosh, "You all catch hold of me and pull!" But as all the khokkosh pulled, their leader's hands slashed open and oceans of black blood streamed onto the floor. Howling demoniacally, the head khokkosh leaped over all the others and ran away.

Another hour passed eventlessly, and Lalkamal began to nod in sleep. He started at a voice outside the door loudly inquiring, "Who's awake in this darkest hour?" By mistake, the sleepy prince began to respond, "Lal's awake and so is . . ." But before he could finish, all the doors and windows of the chamber burst open and a hundred thousand khokkosh leaped upon poor Prince Lal. In the confusion, the oil lamp was doused, and the crown tumbled from Lal's head. Lalkamal called out, "Awake, my brother!"

Neelkamal awoke to find khokkosh all around. Stretching sleepily, he said, "Who dares to break my sleep? Neel and Lal will make them weep!" Upon hearing Neel's voice, the khokkosh became half-dead with fright. Calmly, Neel relit the oil lamp and killed the khokkosh one by one. Then the two brothers washed their hands and faces and went back to sleep.

The next day, the Raja was amazed to find both Princes sleeping peacefully among a hundred thousand slaughtered khokkosh. "Praise be to these Princes who have brought the blessing of peace to our land," cried the grateful King. He promptly handed over his kingdom and the hands of his twin daughters in marriage.

And remember the rakshashi Rani? Well, she was still ruling over her husband's kingdom and soon learned about the massacre of the khokkosh from her reliable rakshash informers. Realizing who must have performed such a feat, she beat her breast and cried,

Ayi-kayi! Oo-hoo!
What ever shall I do?
Oh cursed womb, to bring such woe
The son I bore is now my foe!

She sent two messengers with a single, grim order: "Destroy them!"

Disguised in human form, the rakshash messengers went to the royal court of Lal and Neel. Supplicating themselves before the twin thrones, the messengers said, "Oh, mighty Kings! We have heard of your demon-killing prowess, and have come to beg your aid. Our Raja has taken gravely ill, and cannot be cured without a rakshash's hair-oil. Will you help us obtain this miracle cure?"

After conferring for a moment, Lalkamal and Neelkamal agreed, "We will help our fellow Raja."

Bidding farewell to their twin Ranis, Lal and Neel set out that very evening in search of the magical oil. It soon grew dark, so the brothers tethered their horses to a mighty banyan tree and settled down to rest. Little did they know that very banyan tree was the home of the magical birds Bangama and Bangamee. Later that night, the brothers overheard the birds taking.

Bangamee was telling her husband Bangama, "Aha! Where will we find the kind and brave men who will give us two drops of their blood so that we can cure our babies' blindness?"

Lal and Neel, who prided themselves on their kindness and bravery, called out, "Who is that speaking in the tree? We will give our blood to help your little ones!"

Bangamee cried in happiness, "Aha! Aha!" In the meantime, Bangama came down to meet the young Kings. Although Lal and Neel were tall young men, they were like tiny ants next to the majestic bird. Upon his enormous feathered body, his human face shone with the wisdom of ages. The brothers did not hesitate in piercing their thumbs with their shining daggers and presenting the creature with two drops of royal blood. Bangama took the rubies of blood to his nest, and within moments, the brothers heard a squawking and rustling as two Bangama babies made their way down to the ground.

The baby Bangamas, while small in comparison to their father, were not exactly tiny themselves. Lal and Neel took a cautious step backward as the excited young birds enthusiastically thanked them. "Aha! Aha!" they cried. "Oh, brave Kings, we are indebted to you! How can we repay you for giving us sight? Name any task, and we will do it."

Lal and Neel modestly replied, "Have long and happy lives. Right now, we do not have any task to give you."

The Bangama babies persisted, "Then let us carry you to your destination." Not able to refuse such an offer, Lal and Neel climbed onto the backs of the gigantic birds. Soon, they were airborne. Earth and forests, oceans and rivers, mountains

and hills, even clouds were left behind as the Bangama flapped
their mighty wings toward the Demon-Land. After seven days
and seven nights of flight, they landed upon a mountain. Beneath the mountain stretched a deep valley, and beyond the
valley was the land of the rakshash. Although enormous and
magical creatures, the Bangama were still babies, and as you
know, killing demons is a far too dangerous task for youngsters. So Lalkamal and Neelkamal bid the Bangama goodbye,
and made their way down the mountain by foot.

As they walked, Neelkamal picked some seeds from a tree
and gave them to Lal. "Dada," he said, "hide these sweet lentil
seeds in your pocket, and if someone asks you to chew on iron
pellets, chew on these instead." Then, as soon as the brothers
had crossed the valley, they heard.

Haau! Maau! Khauu!
It's human flesh I smell!
With curry leaves and turmeric
let's cook the rascals well!

Within moments, Lal and Neel were surrounded by hundreds
and thousands of rakshash, all of whom were stretching out
their wicked claws to catch them. Keeping his wits about him,
Neel yelled out, "Ayi-Ma, Ayi-Ma! We have come, your grand-
sons, to see you!"

"Stop! Stop!" cried out a voice. With bony arms a-waving,
monstrous feet a-stomping, and knotty hair twisting this way
and that, an old rakshashi crone came galumphing out of the
crowd. "Oh, my little Neelu babu! Oh, my shriveled bean-pole!
Oh, my scrawny crow grandbaby!" she crooned, while clutching Neelkamal to her breast. Eyeing Lalkamal greedily, the crone
slurped, "And who's this scrumptious morsel you've brought
with you?"

"He's my brother, Ayi-Ma," explained Neel hurriedly.

"Then why does he smell like a human pup?" asked the crone.
"If he is my grandson true, here's some iron pellets for him to
chew!" With these words, the crone snorted out a handful of
iron pellets from her nostrils and handed them to Lal.

143

If you'll remember, Neel had warned his brother about just such a situation. So Lal deftly hid the iron pellets and substituted them with the sweet lentil seeds from his pocket. Hearing Lal crunching and munching on the seeds noisily, the rakshashi was convinced. She held Lal and Neel in a near suffocating embrace and sang,

I am Ayi-Ma
Mother of mother
For Lalu and Neelu
there is no other.

But the smell of Lalkamal's human flesh was too much for the crone. Her eyes turned glassy with hunger and her tongue poured out seven oceans of drool. But this was her grandson, how could she eat him? The rakshashi crone had to control herself. She carried her beloved grandbabies all the way home.

What a kingdom was Demon-Land! Every square mile was teeming with ferocious, hungry rakshash. And to ensure variety in their menus, they had filled their kingdom with every species of animal on earth. From the crone's arms, Lal and Neel witnessed the rotting carcasses, the wanton destruction of lives. Lalkamal whispered to his brother, "The earth will soon be empty from the rakshash's greed!"

That night, when the nocturnal rakshash had left for the hunt, Lal and Neel traveled to a well on the south side of the kingdom. Neel instructed his brother to keep an eye out for danger while he climbed down into the dark well. In a little while, he emerged with a dagger and a tiny golden box. Upon opening the box, the brothers saw two black hornets, Jiyan and Maran. Jiyan was the keeper of all rakshash life, while Maran was the keeper of one particular life—that of the rakshashi Rani. As soon as the box was opened and the hornets were touched by the night air, all the rakshash began to feel ill. Heads spinning, hearts pounding, they ran pell-mell from all corners of the world back to their homeland. In her kingdom, the rakshashi Rani was so sick that she collapsed with weakness.

When Neelkamal ripped off the back legs of Jiyan, the legs

144

of all the rakshash fell off. This, however, did not stop them. Being a resourceful species, the rakshash continued running on their hands. When Neel ripped off the front limbs of the hornet, all the rakshash lost their arms. Still, they kept coming. Now, Neelkamal took the dagger he had found in the well and cut off the bee's head. The rakshash stopped dead in their tracks as their enormous heads rolled off their demonic bodies. Demon-Land became empty, without a soul.

But there was one rakshash left to contend with. Lal and Neel took the hornet Maran and called to their feathered friends: "Bangam! Bangam!" Immediately, the baby Bangama arrived at the brothers' side and carried them toward home. After three months and thirteen nights, Lal and Neel returned to their kingdom. "Where are those messengers who had requested our aid?" they asked. But, as Lal and Neel had guessed, the rakshash messengers had vanished.

In the meantime, the rakshashi Rani, being a very powerful demon, had sensed that her soul was in the possession of Lal and Neel. Gathering all her strength, and throwing off her human disguise, the Rani ran toward the brothers' kingdom in her true rakshash form. Eyes rolling, teeth gnashing, claws bared, she yelled as she ran,

Warm flesh, warm flesh
Toasty, crisp and sweet!
I'll suck their marrow, chew their bones
and curry up their feet!
With great delight, I will light
their burning funeral pyre!
Dance in glee, pour some ghee
and watch the flames go higher!

When the Rani had reached the outskirts of the kingdom, Lalkamal opened the golden box and took out the hornet Maran. Seeing her soul in Lal's hands, the rakshashi stood trembling in fear. Without further ado, Lal killed the hornet with the magic dagger, and the rakshashi Rani was immediately destroyed.

With the death of the rakshashi Rani, the spell that had been put upon the paralyzed Raja was broken. Waking, he mourned, "Oh, where are my sons?" Lal and Neel, the two brothers, knelt before their father and touched his feet. Confusedly, the Raja asked, "Are you my Ajit and Kusum?"

In one voice, the kingdom replied, "Yes, these are our Princes!" The two realms now became one. Reunited with their wives, the kings Lalkamal and Neelkamal spent the rest of their days together in happiness.

THE BRAHMAN GHOST

There was once a Brahman who was so poor that he could not afford to marry. Yet, his mother had no greater wish than for him to take a wife, so that she could have company when he was away. As you know, in those days, a man had to pay a hefty bride-price for a wife. So, to fulfill his mother's dearest wish, the poor Brahman went from door to door, asking the neighboring villagers to help him raise money for his wedding. Soon, he had enough gold to marry.

But fortune did not shine upon the poor Brahman even after he brought his wife home. He soon realized that he did not have enough money to support his family properly. He went to his mother and said, "Ma, I cannot afford to feed you and my new bou. I must go abroad and earn some money. It might be a long time before I return, since I have vowed not to come home until I am rich. What little I have, I leave with you. You must try to manage on this pittance and look after my bou as well."

With these words the Brahman touched his mother's feet to ask for her blessings, bid farewell to his wife, and was on his way.

That very evening, a ghost came to the house disguised in the Brahman's form. Believing him to be her husband, the Brahman's new bride exclaimed, "What's this? You've come back so soon? I thought you said you might be gone for a few years! Did you change your mind?"

The ghost replied, "Today is such a beautiful day, I decided to return home. Besides, I have been able to earn a little money."

Neither the Brahman's wife nor his mother suspected anything. The ghost slipped into the Brahman's life, becoming the head of his household, the beloved son of his mother, the husband of his new bride. So similar looking was the specter to the Brahman, the neighboring villagers accepted the ghost as well.

A few years went by. Finally, the true Brahman returned to his home. To his amazement, he found someone else had taken his place! Seeing another man wearing his own face and form, he was thunderstruck.

Seeing the Brahman, the ghost coolly asked, "And who are you? What business do you have in my home?"

"Who am I?" exclaimed the amazed Brahman. "I could ask you the same question! This is my home; that is my mother; and there is my wife."

The ghost replied, "Indeed! That is the most ridiculous thing I have ever heard. Everyone knows, this is my house, my bou and my ma. I have been living here for so many years! You can't suddenly show up from nowhere and claim that this is your mother, wife and house. My dear Brahman, you have gone mad." He promptly kicked the Brahman out of his own home.

At these astounding events, the Brahman was speechless. What was he to do now? At last he decided to approach the Raja for help.

When the Raja called both men to his court, he rubbed his eyes in astonishment. Was he seeing double? Although a wise adjudicator, the Raja could not fathom how he would solve this controversy. He announced that he would need time to think over the problem.

The Brahman's tears flowed freely. "What a sinful world this is! An impostor has taken over my household, stolen the love of my mother and wife, and the Raja does nothing! What kind of justice is this?"

Every day, the Brahman appeared before the Raja, pleading piteously for justice. And every day the Raja said, "Come tomorrow."

*　　*　　*

Each day, after visiting the palace, the Brahman would pass by the field where the village cattle grazed.

While the animals fed, the young cowherds played games to pass the time. Their favorite game was playing King. One particular boy, Rakhal, was the natural leader of the group, and he was usually selected to play the Raja.

One day, when the Brahman was returning from court, he was approached by a cowherd. "Our Raja commands your presence."

The confused Brahman replied, "I have only just left the royal court. Why must I return again?"

Explained the boy, "It is our Rakhal Raja who wants you!"

The Brahman followed the boy out of sheer curiosity. As he approached an enormous banyan tree, he saw the young cowherd king holding court beneath the shady boughs. Rakhal motioned majestically for the Brahman to approach him. "I am curious, good Brahman," he queried, "why do you weep every day as you pass this field?"

Amused at the young boy's imperiousness, the Brahman decided to indulge him. He told his sorrowful tale to the groups of attentive cowherds. Rakhal listened carefully until the Brahman was finished. He then declared, "Do not fear, good Brahman, I will solve your problem. But first, you must do something for me. I am only the King of the cowherds, and have no real power. You must approach the Raja and ask him to make me a royal judge. Only then can I help you."

The Brahman was caught between disbelief and hope. The young man was so confident, could he really find a solution? Thinking that he had nothing to lose, the Brahman requested the Raja to allow this favor. The Raja readily agreed, quite pleased to be rid of the difficult dilemma.

Newly empowered as a royal judge, Rakhal the cowherd summoned both Brahmans to his banyan tree courtroom. He asked each of the two men to show cause why theirs was the true claim. The ghostly Brahman presented an endless number of witnesses to his identity, including his wife and mother. The actual Brahman, having been away for so many years, could provide no such support. He was armed only with the conviction in his heart and the truth of his words.

After hearing all of the testimony, Rakhal held up a hand.

"Enough, I will hear no more," he cried, "I have a final test that will settle the argument once and for all." With these words, he drew forth a small glass bottle with a long, narrow neck. He declared, "Whichever of you can enter this glass bottle will be hereby pronounced the true Brahman."

The Brahman was aghast. "What kind of justice is this? How can you expect me to enter that glass bottle?"

Rakhal was unmoved. "If you cannot, then you must not be the true Brahman. Let me ask your opponent." He gestured to the other man, "Can you, Sir, pass this test and prove your identity?"

Elated at the thought of imminent victory, the ghostly Brahman exclaimed, "Yes, of course! What a simple task!" He promptly turned into a puff of smoke and entered the bottle.

Without further ado, Rakhal corked the bottle and the tricky ghost was trapped forever.

Handing the bottle over to the Brahman, Rakhal said, "Throw this into the ocean, good Brahman, and you will never be bothered by the ghost again. I have given my judgment, and kept my promise to you. Go now to your family."

From them on, the Brahman lived happily with his wife and mother. He had many fine children who cared for him in his old age.

The Raja was so pleased with the cowherd Rakhal's handling of the case that he made him a royal minister. As a minister, Rakhal grew to be respected all over the kingdom for his wisdom and fair judgments.

THE GHOSTLY WIFE

There once was a poor villager who lived in a tiny hut with his young wife and his mother. The hut was located at the very outskirts of the village, by an enormous pond. On the east bank of the pond grew many jackfruit trees, and in the tallest of these trees lived a shakchunni. Every evening, when the village women came to the pond to fetch water, the shakchunni would watch wistfully from her jackfruit perch. As you know, shakchunnis are the ghosts of married women who have died accidentally, and so their greatest wish is to once again become wives. This particular shakchunni wanted nothing more.

One evening, when the wife of the poor villager was returning from the pond with a brimming pitcher, she clumsily splashed some water on the shakchunni. Furious, the ghost whisked the unfortunate woman into a dark hollow of her jackfruit tree. Slipping into the wife's sari and shell bangles, balancing the pitcher of water expertly on her waist, the shakchunni gleefully headed toward the poor villager's hut. So clever was the ghost's disguise that neither the villager nor his mother realized there was anything amiss.

The next day, however, the mother-in-law began to suspect that there was something a little different about her son's wife. While her daughter-in-law had once been slow and lazy, taking all day to complete a single chore, she was now finishing all her household tasks in the blink of an eye. The old woman rejoiced, "Finally, my daughter-in-law has learned her wifely duties."

But as days went by, the mother-in-law became more and more amazed by the younger woman's swiftness. She would cook the day's meals, clean the hut, and fetch water all before the morning had even passed. When the old woman wanted something from the next room, the object would appear even before the words were out of her mouth. What she didn't realize was that her shakchunni daughter-in-law could extend her ghostly arms without moving. Thus, the shakchunni wife would complete a task faster than the mother-in-law could speak.

Then, the mother-in-law noticed a very bizarre incident. One evening, when sitting down for his dinner, the villager asked for a slice of lime with his rice. Without moving, the shakchunni wife extended her arm out the window, picked a fresh lime from a nearby tree, and brought the fruit back to the kitchen. Although the son didn't notice anything, being too busy with the steaming meal before him, the mother-in-law's eyes widened with fear. Later, when the young wife was busy washing dishes, the old woman drew her son aside and recounted what she had seen. Together, they decided that they would have to keep a watchful eye on the new bride.

One morning, before preparing the day's meals, the mother-in-law noticed that there was no fuel left in the tiny hut. As she headed out to gather some firewood, she glanced back through the kitchen window and witnessed a frightening sight. There, a pot of rice was boiling merrily over a blazing fire. Rather than using wood, the young wife had stuck her own two feet into the stove and set them aflame. The old woman ran straight to the fields where her son was working and informed him. "That cannot be our bou, my son, it must be a shakchunni or petni!"

The old woman and her son went to fetch the village ojha. The ojha declared, "The first thing we must do is to discover whether this woman is truly a ghost." He lit a piece of turmeric and let its smell permeate the villager's hut. As you know, neither shakchunnis nor any other kind of ghost can tolerate the odor of burning turmeric. To them, it is the worst kind of torture. So, when the villager's wife began howling about the awful stink in the house, no one had a doubt as to her identity.

Then, the ojha began his real work. He took a handful of mustard seeds, said an incantation over them, and threw them at the shakchunni. The seeds were like little arrows on the ghost's skin. Still holding her nose, she let out a blood-curdling scream as the seeds struck her body. Returning to her shakchunni form, she piteously begged the ojha to stop. But the ojha had no mercy for such sneaky ghosts and continued to pelt the shakchunni with the incanted seeds. He declared, "I won't stop until you bring back the actual bou of this house! What have you done with her?"

The shakchunni screeched in her nasal, ghostly voice, "I punished the young bride for splashing me with water. I took her away." She shrieked at the villager, "Your wife is in the hollow of the jackfruit tree! I'll set her free! Now let me be!"

Of course, the ojha would hear none of this, and wisely advised the villager to rescue his wife before they released the shakchunni. When the villager returned with his true wife, the ojha made the shakchunni promise never to trouble anyone in the village again.

The shakchunni was as good as her word, and did not bother anyone ever again. After recovering her health, the young wife happily tended her home and was careful about her duties. She and the villager had many healthy children, who listened wide-eyed to their grandmother tell tales of the ghost who had once stolen their mother.

THE DEMON QUEEN

There were once a King's son, a minister's son, a merchant's son and a general's son who were great friends. The four compatriots would travel the countryside together in search of adventure. One day, they decided to see the world beyond their kingdom. So they mounted their horses and galloped away over mountains and valleys, fields and meadows.

After a long day's journey, they came upon a dark and gloomy forest. The minister's son noticed that there were no birds singing in the trees, neither was there evidence of any woodland creatures. "Friends," he said, "this forest seems very strange and ominous. Let us not stop here, but travel on a little further."

But the others laughed at his fears. "We are four brave young men, who can harm us?" exclaimed the general's son. "Do not worry. Besides, we are all very tired. Let us rest here for the night."

So the four friends tethered their horses and started making preparations for camp. The merchant's son worried, "What will we eat?"

Just then, the Prince, who was called Roop Kumar, spotted a fresh stag's head lying some distance away. "A hunter must have left it there," he exclaimed. "Let us make it our dinner tonight."

His friends cheered happily, "Thanks to you, we have found something to fill our bellies. Now that you have done your part, we will do ours."

Leaving Roop Kumar to rest, the three friends headed into the dark forest. The minister's son was to fetch water, the merchant's son was to collect firewood, and the general's son was to gather fruits to eat. Prince Roop laid down upon a grassy patch and promptly fell asleep.

In a little while, the merchant's son returned with an armload of firewood. He put down the sticks without waking Roop Kumar, then thought to himself, "Let me clean the meat before the others return." But the moment he picked up the stag's head, it turned into a fearsome rakshashi and swallowed him whole. Before the merchant's son could even call for help, he was eaten up, and the rakshashi had turned back into the stag's head.

A little while later, the general's son came back with his quiver full of fruits. He saw the firewood, and thought to himself, "Perhaps my friend has wandered off. I will start preparing the meal." He put down the fruits and went toward the stag's head. As soon as he touched it, he too was swallowed up by the ferocious rakshashi.

Soon after, the minister's son returned with a pitcherful of water. When he spotted the fruits and firewood, he felt a twinge of suspicion. Placing his brimming pitcher beside the sleeping Prince, he wondered, "Where have my friends gone?" Then, he too went to collect the stag's head. Immediately, the rakshashi took her demonic form and reached out her vicious talons to catch him. Unable to defend himself against the enormous monster, the minister's son yelled out, "Roop! Awake, friend! Run! Run! Save yourself!"

Startled, Roop Kumar awoke to see his friend being devoured by a fierce rakshashi. Without pausing for a moment, he began to run as fast as his legs could carry him. As he dashed through the dark countryside, Prince Roop could hear the rakshashi flying after him. The poor Prince could feel his legs giving out, his breath catching at his throat. Yet the rakshashi pursued him relentlessly. When he felt he could run no longer, Roop Kumar fell to his knees before a tall mango tree and begged, "Please, ancient tree, save this poor mortal."

Hearing his gracious appeal, the mango tree promptly parted and enveloped the Prince within its trunk. When the rakshashi arrived, she pleaded, wheedled, argued and threatened, but the tree did not yield her charge. Finally, the demon changed herself into a lovely maiden and sat down beneath the tree, weeping copiously.

It so happened that the King of that very kingdom was hunting the next day in the forest. When he spotted the sobbing beauty, his heart melted. He immediately married the distressed damsel, and took her home to his palace.

*　　*　　*

The rakshashi now became Queen of the realm. She would spend her long days in the palace planning how to catch the tasty Prince that got away.

One day, the rakshashi Queen placed a pallet of reeds under her mattress. As she tossed and turned upon the bed, the reeds made dreadful crackling noises that filled the halls of the palace. All the courtiers guessed that the Queen must have contracted a dreadful disease for her bones to be cracking so.

When the King learned of his new wife's illness, he ran to her side. "My dear, what is wrong?" he exclaimed.

The Queen replied in a tremulous voice, "I have contracted bone-crackitis, and my very skeleton is dissolving inside me."

The poor King had never heard of this awful disease, but when he heard the reeds crackle, he knew it was something very serious indeed. He summoned all the best doctors and medicine men of the land, but his wife did not recover.

Finally, the Queen declared, "In the forest, there is a mango tree that grows tall by a lake. You must chop down that tree and burn it in the palace garden beneath my window. I will get better only when I inhale that smoke."

Promptly, hundreds of royal woodcutters were dispatched to chop down the mango tree. The Prince, who was still hiding within the trunk, requested, "Oh, generous tree, you have protected me for so long. Please put me inside one of the sweet fruits that hangs from your branches, and drop me into the lake."

The woodcutters failed to notice a tiny mango falling from the tree into the depths of the lake. A carp that was swimming by happily swallowed the fruit whole.

156

In the meantime, the mango tree was burned in the garden beneath the Queen's window. But to her husband's disappointment, there was no improvement in her health. The rakshashi knew the Prince had escaped again. She had to devise another plan to catch her enemy. This time, she told the King, "There is a huge carp that swims in the lake. I will only get well when I eat the sweet mango that rests in its stomach."

Immediately, hundreds of royal fishermen threw down their strongest nets into the lake. Along with all the other fish, the giant carp was captured. The Prince pleaded with the carp, "Respected fish, you know this poor mortal's troubles and have protected me for so long. Please put me in an oyster's shell and throw me to the bottom of the lake."

When the fishermen brought the carp's mango to the Queen, she ate it with gusto. However, she still made no recovery. As soon as she tasted it, the rakshashi realized there was no Prince within the fruit.

The King continued to grieve over the bone-crackitis that afflicted his beloved wife.

*　　*　　*

One day, a villager's wife had gone to the lake to bathe and stepped upon a sharp oyster shell. When she picked it up and threw it away, the shell broke apart and a magnificent Prince emerged. The young wife trembled in fear, "What have I done? This must be some divine being!"

Roop Kumar assured her, "Do not fear, good wife. I am but a mortal Prince who was trapped within an oyster shell to escape a rakshashi's clutches. I am indebted to you for releasing me. You are my friend for life." Prince Roop began living with the villager and his wife in their humble cottage.

In the palace, the rakshashi Queen realized this development. She gnashed her teeth in anger at missing the Prince again. She called the King to her bedside and said, "I will never recover unless you get the ever-blooming champak flower, the dancing stick, the softest reed pallet, and the magic twelve-guage squash which bears a single thirteen-guage seed."

When the King asked his wife where he should find such things, she explained, "In my ancestors' house."

But who was to be appointed to bring these items? Said the Queen, "There is a certain Prince hiding in a villager's hut. No one but that young man can bring my cure."

Hundreds of royal soldiers were dispatched that minute to the village. Although Roop Kumar tried to escape, they captured him quickly and brought him back to the palace. Prince Roop prostrated himself before the King and begged, "Sire, your Queen is a rakshashi. Please save this humble Prince from her wrath."

The King's eyes flashed in anger. "That is a terrible lie!" He boomed, "You must retrieve from her ancestral home the ever-blooming champak flower, the dancing stick, the soft pallet and the magic squash. If you do not comply, I will attack your father's kingdom with my fiercest armies!"

What else could Roop do? He set off for the rakshashi Queen's home. After traveling for many days and nights, he arrived before an enormous palace. But when he stepped inside, he could not see a single living soul. He wandered through the palace hoping to find someone. Finally, in a remote room, he found an enchanting Princess sleeping upon a bed of gold. He tried to awaken the beautiful maiden, but all his efforts were in vain. The Princess would not wake! Prince Roop realized she must be under some sort of spell.

Then Roop Kumar noticed a silver stick near the princess's pillow, and a golden stick resting near her feet. On a whim, he took the gold stick and placed it by her fair face, then put the silver stick at her delicate feet.

Immediately, the young maiden opened her doe-like eyes and exclaimed, "Who are you, Sir? Are you man, monster, or god? Whatever you be, you must run away at once. This is the palace of rakshash!"

Answered Prince Roop, "Don't worry, dear Princess. I am a mortal Prince who is being chased by a fierce rakshashi Queen." Quickly, he explained to the maiden all that had occurred.

Then the Princess told Roop her story. "This palace is actually my father's," she said sadly. "When the terrible rakshash

158

attacked, they devoured my parents. But one old rakshashi crone took a liking to me, and decided to keep me prisoner as her granddaughter. Every evening, when the rakshash go to hunt, she puts me under a sleeping spell with the gold and silver sticks."

Before she had finished speaking, the Prince and Princess heard a terrible din. The rakshash were returning!

Ayi-lo! Mai-lo! Is that human flesh I smell?
We'll tear his limbs, eat him up, then ring his death-knell!

The Princess shivered in fear for Roop. She urged, "Put me back to sleep! Then go hide in the Shiva temple, under the flower offerings! The rakshash will never enter a place of worship!"

In a little while, the maiden was awakened again, this time by the rakshashi crone. The old rakshashi asked her, "Why do I smell human flesh, my pretty? Did you have a little visitor?"

"Where would I find human people?" asked the wide-eyed Princess. "You must be smelling me, dearest Ayi-Ma. If you must, why don't you have me for supper?"

"Oh no, no!" exclaimed the crone. "How can I eat my little adopted grandbaby? Look, my pretty one, at all the nice food I have brought for you!"

After feeding the Princess dinner, the crone and all the other rakshash poured gallons of mustard oil into their nostrils and ears, put blankets over their faces, and fell asleep. The poor maiden stayed awake all night, plucking gray hairs from the crone's greasy head.

The next day, the crone put the sleeping spell upon the Princess again before leaving for the hunt. As soon as the rakshash had left, Prince Roop emerged from the Shiva temple and awakened the lovely maiden. The happy couple spent their day wandering in the garden, playing pasha, and enjoying each other's company. Finally, Roop asked, "How long can we go on like this? Today, when the crone returns, you must find out from her where the rakshash store their souls."

That evening, when the rakshash returned, Roop Kumar hid

himself again in the temple. After feeding the Princess her dinner, the old rakshashi crone was leaning back upon the bed. The clever Princess wheedled, "Oh, most vicious Ayi-Ma, you have trampled all over the world today. You have ransacked so many villages, attacked so many kingdoms, you must be exhausted. Let me cool your brow with this hand-fan and rub your weary feet."

"Oh, what a good little grandbaby!" exclaimed the rakshashi. "Even if you are a human! Pillaging and plundering are hard on these weary old bones, and my feet are aching terribly. Won't you press them for me?"

"Of course, my fearsome Ayi-Ma!" effused the Princess. She poured a bucket of mustard oil upon the old crone's gruesome clawed feet and began massaging them. As she went about her task, the Princess slyly dabbed some of the stinging oil into her own eyes to make herself cry. One of the Princess's teardrops fell upon the crone's calloused feet.

The startled rakshashi took the teardrop upon one taloned finger and tasted it. She exclaimed, "What's this, little grandbaby? Why do you cry these salty tears? With your loving Ayi-Ma around, what reason do you have to be sad?"

"I'm crying, Ayi-Ma, because someday you will die, and then all the other rakshash will eat me!" wailed the clever Princess.

"Why should I die, my scrawny grandbaby? There's nothing in this world that can kill your vicious Ayi-Ma!" The rakshashi continued, "There is a marble pillar beneath that yonder pond. Inside that column is a snake with seven hoods. If a Prince can climb a palm tree, pick a sharp leaf, dive under the water, break the mighty pillar, capture the poisonous snake and then cut it to pieces with a palm-leaf sword, only then will I be killed! And he must accomplish all of this in one breath!" The crone cackled gleefully, "But remember, grandbaby, from each drop of snake's blood that falls upon the earth, seven thousand rakshash will be born! So you see, there's no need to fear for me."

The Princess sighed in relief, "That's comforting news, Ayi-Ma. That means you will never die." She continued to massage the crone's warted feet for a little longer. Then, she casually asked, "Tell me, Ayi-Ma, the rakshashi Queen of that yonder land—where is her soul kept? And where can someone find the ever-blooming champak, the soft reed pallet, the dancing sticks and the squash with a seed longer than itself?"

"Oh, you curious grandchild!" said the crone. "There is a tia that lives in a tower room of this very palace. The rakshashi Queen's soul is housed in that bird." As the old rakshashi's eyes drooped in sleep, she continued, "And those precious objects are in this palace as well. I will give them to you tomorrow to play with."

The next day, before the rakshash left for their hunt, the crone gave the Princess the magic items. "Don't worry, grandbaby, today we will not go far," assured the rakshashi. Then she put the maiden to sleep and left.

When Roop Kumar awakened her, the fair Princess said, "We have much time today, for the rakshash will be returning very late."

"How do you know this?" inquired the Prince.

The Princess answered with a laugh, "Simple. When a rakshash says he is staying nearby, he is actually going very far. When he says he is going far, he will really do the opposite!"

And so, Roop Kumar began his task of destroying the rakshash souls. Holding his breath, he climbed to the top of a tall palm tree and picked its sharpest leaf. With a mighty leap, he then dived from the tree into the pond, broke the marble column, grabbed the seven-hooded serpent and rose to the surface.

Sensing that their souls were in jeopardy, all the rakshash began clamoring toward home. Prince Roop quickly placed the serpent upon his chest, so that no poisonous blood could drop to the earth, and killed the snake with one swift blow. All the rakshash fell dead wherever they were.

In the meantime, the Princess had gathered all the magic items that the crone had left her. She ran to the palace tower and found the magic tia bird as well. Said Prince Roop, "Dearest lady, you must accompany me to the rakshashi Queen's palace."

Once at the King's court, Roop Kumar presented the monarch with the champak flower, pallet, sticks and squash, saying, "Maharaj, the Queen herself must come to collect these items."

Anticipating her speedy recovery, the jubilant King sent for his wife at once. By that time, the rakshashi Queen had figured out that all her kin had been killed. In a blind rage, she transformed into her demonic form and charged into the court. Her eyes blazed, her tongue lolled and her claws grabbed for Prince Roop Kumar. The courtiers trembled in fear and the King hid behind the throne. But the moment the Queen spied the tia bird in Roop's hands, she stopped in her tracks. In her sweetest voice, she reasoned, "Please don't touch the bird, give it to me. I won't bother any of you again."

Prince Roop demanded, "In that case, you must return to me my friends, the minister's son, the merchant's son and the general's son. You must also return our four horses."

Promptly, the frightened rakshashi spit out all that he had called for. As the four reunited friends were joyously embracing each other, the demon Queen rushed at them with one final swoop. Swiftly, Roop Kumar killed the rakshashi's soul-bearing bird. And that was the end of the demon Queen.

The grateful King rewarded the four friends handsomely. Then the Prince, Princess, minister's son, merchant's son and general's son all returned to their own kingdom. There was a grand welcome for the returning heroes. Roop Kumar and the Princess were soon married, and lived happily with their parents in the royal palace.

And forever more, for all time to come, in the future of the universe, there were no more rakshash upon the earth!

COME, OH SLEEP
(a bedtime rhyme)

Come, oh sleep, come
I'll give you honeyed milk
Come, oh sleep, come
I'll give you soft spun silk
Come, oh sleep, come
I'll give you sweets to eat
Come to my baby's eyes
and place your golden seat

GLOSSARY

Apsara: Mythical female creatures who enchant humans with their beauty, singing and dancing

Aryan: A Caucasian group that invaded India during the second millennium B.C.

Ashok: A large tree

Ayi-Ma: Grandmother; literally, mother of mother

Baba: Father

Bangama (m), Bangamee (f): Enormous and wise mythological birds; usually conceived as having human faces

Baro: Eldest

Betel tree: A tree in the palm family that bears the edible betel-nuts

Bhoot: Ghosts; categorized according to their personality, caste, gender and religion in mortal life

Bou: Wife, bride

Brahman: A person of the highest caste among Hindus: often a priest or a teacher

Chaitra: A month in the Bengali calendar; around March

Champak, Parul, Malati, Rajanigandha: Fragrant flowers

Choto: Youngest

Conch: Shell of the conch mollusk; makes a wailing sound when one blows into it

Dacoit: Robber

Dada: Elder brother

Devata: Gods in their anthropomorphized forms

Devi: The essential goddess; has many manifestations, including Uma, Parvati, Kali and Durga

Didi: Elder sister

Dravidians: Indigenous people of prehistoric India, primarily from the southern region

Doyel: A singing bird

Ganges: The Hindu holy river flowing through West Bengal

Gauri: An incarnation of the Hindu goddess Devi; daughter of Himalaya, wife of Shiva

Ghee: Clarified butter

Hiremon: A small mythological bird

164

Hoogly: A district neighboring Calcutta
Howdah: A chair-like saddle placed on elephants
Indra: The king of gods in the Hindu pantheon
Jiyan: Life
Kamal: Lotus
Khokkosh: An animal-like demon, not as powerful as a rakshash
Khokon: Young boy
Kurma: Vegetables prepared with sesame and nuts
Lal: Red
Ma: Mother
Maharaj: Great king
Mahout: One who guides/drives elephants
Mama: Mother's brother
Mami: Mama's wife
Maran: Death
Maya: Illusion
Moghul: Islamic invaders who came to India from Persia; their Delhi-based empire was founded around the 16th century A.D.
Moshai: Address equivalent to "Sir"
Natai-Chandi: A folk goddess
Naute: Edible thorny leafy greens
Neel: Blue
Ojha: Exorcist
Pahar: Mountain
Pakkhiraj: The mythological winged horse
Pan: Betel leaf; a mouth freshener, usually eaten after meals with betel nuts
Pasha: An ancient board game, similar to checkers
Pathans: Islamic invaders who came to India from the region that is now Afghanistan; their Delhi-based empire was founded around the 12th century A.D.
Payas: Rice pudding
Petni: Ghost of a woman
Puja: Act of worship
Pulao: A rice preparation made with ghee and nuts
Raja: King
Rakhal: Cowherd
Rakshash (m), Rakshashi (f): A demon-like creature
Ram: Hero of the ancient Indian epic, *Ramayana*
Rani: Queen
Rui, Katla: Freshwater fish
Rupee: The Indian currency
Sandalwood: A fragrant wood
Sanyasi: A Hindu holy man
Sepoy: Indian soldiers during the British Raj

Shakchunni: Ghost of a young married woman

Shashti: The sixth day of a lunar cycle; also the folk-goddess of fertility and children

Shishu, Debdaru: Slim and tall tropical trees that look like poplars

Shiva: A Hindu god

Tamarind: A sour fruit

Tia: Parrot

Tulsi: A small plant considered holy and used in rituals; similar to sweet basil

Tuntuni: A small bird, similar to a hummingbird

Vermilion: A red powder, used by Hindu Bengali women on their forehead to denote marriage; also used in other rituals for good luck

REFERENCES

Bandopadhyaye, R. (1987). *Bangalar Itihas (History of Bengal)* (Vols. 1 & 2). Calcutta: Dey's Publishing. (*In Bengali.*)

Beck, B. E. F., Claus, P. J., Goswami, P., & Handoo, J. (1987). *Folktales of India.* Chicago: University of Chicago Press.

Day, L. B. (1883). *Folktales of Bengal.* Calcutta: Book Society of India, Ltd.

Organ, T. W. (1974). *Hinduism: Its Historic Development.* Woodbury, NY: Barron's Educational Series, Inc.

Roy, M. (1972). *Bengali Women.* Chicago: University of Chicago Press.

Wolpert, S. (1989). *A New History of India.* New York: Oxford University Press.